Goddess of the Moon

Text copyright ©2012 by Glenda Reynolds

All rights reserved. Except as permitted under the U.S. Copyright Act of 1976, no part of this publication may be reproduced, distributed, or transmitted in any form or by any means, or stored in a database, or retrieval system, without the prior written permission of the author.

This is a work of fiction. Any resemblance of characters to actual persons, living or dead, is purely coincidental. The author holds exclusive rights to this work. Unauthorized duplication is prohibited.

Goddess of the Moon: Mayan World of Vampires

ISBN-13: 978-1478173656

Printed in the United States of America

To Linda and Rebecca Skipper for giving me advise and encouraging me on this journey.

To my husband, Bob, my love and my best friend 29 years and counting, thanks for believing in me and seeing what others don't see in me.

CONTENTS

1. THE DARK ONE — 3
2. THE GOLDEN AGE — 10
3. GIRLS JUST WANNA HAVE FUN — 16
4. WOMEN'S RITE OF PASSAGE — 26
5. AN UNEXPECTED GUEST — 31
6. SIBLING RIVALRY — 40
7. THE STRANGER CAME KNOCKING — 51
8. BONFIRE NIGHT — 64
9. ESCAPING REALITY — 71
10. TEZ'S SECRET REVEALED — 80
11. ZAFRINA'S INVITATION — 87
12. THE RESISTANCE REVEALED — 97
13. TRAINING DAY BEGINS — 111
14. THE ENEMY WITHIN — 120
15. HOW DO I HATE THEE? LET ME COUNT THE WAYS — 129
16. GRUDGINGLY MAKING PREPARATIONS — 148
17. THE BALLCOURT GAMES — 163
18. THE WEDDING DAY — 173
19. THE FIGHT FOR FREEDOM — 185
20. THE AFTERMATH — 200

EPILOGUE - THE NEW WORLD — 216

Goddess of the Moon
MAYAN WORLD OF VAMPIRES

Glenda Reynolds

CreateSpace, DBA On-Demand Publishing, LLC

1. THE DARK ONE

In the Mayan city of Coba, near the Eastern coast of the Yucatan, the people gathered in the sweltering heat at the foot of the pyramid. The pyramid was erected in honor of the Dark One, Zafrina, Goddess of the Moon. The seven level structure was the tallest one in Southeastern Mexico. From the top of it, one could see a carpet of lush green jungle as far as the eye could see. But there were no people present that appreciated such beauty or celebrated life. They were summoned there as it were to witness things that went against the conscience of the average man, woman or child. Things that should make one's skin crawl or shake with fear.

The pyramid was impressive to see with its open temple and stately columns at the top. It was unique in design, although Zafrina had used many different pyramids in other lands for this very purpose.

There were several platforms at varied heights parallel to the pyramid where people participated in bloodletting rituals such as piercing their skin on different parts of their bodies. They pierced their tongues with barbed rope. Women in scant clothing swayed to the beat of drums while their eyes rolled back in their heads. Tiny babies, just days old, were sacrificed to fulfill the bloodlust of the Dark One. Their peaceful faces peeked out from their blood stained swaddling clothes as they lay on top of some of the sacrificial platforms. The mothers were proud that their little ones were counted worthy for sacrifice. People are like sheep. They can be so quick to believe a lie. They could even play into the hands of one as seductive and powerful as Zafrina.

The sun was slowly sinking in the horizon. It would soon be time.

Princess Melanna stood with her closest friends on a platform that was parallel to the pyramid that reached two thirds of its height. They had a better view of what was happening than those at the bottom of the pyramid.

As the last rays of the golden sun disappeared, the Dark One and her servants, known as the Ancients, lead a procession on the top of the pyramid. Their torches blazed as they followed behind her in two rows. All were wearing ornamental masks and dark robes. Zafrina's mask was decorated with more detail in turquoise, orange argillite and feather plumes. She wore a silver talisman around her neck that permitted her to walk in the sunlight without dying. It was also inlaid with the turquoise and orange argillite in the shape of a crescent moon.

In between the Ancients was a sullen young man, clothed from the hips down; his face was cast down in shadows. He stood taller than his captors with the glow of youth and a broad build. As they approached in plainer view, the young man, Noctli, lifted his face to the crowd. On his face was the look of despair as tears streamed down his cheeks. His demeanor changed when he half smiled with glazed eyes, as if he had wildly anticipated this moment.

Zafrina possessed great Power both over humans and the natural elements. Noctli's friends were unaware that he had been easily compelled by Zafrina to do her bidding and give himself for a human sacrifice.

Melanna and her friends let out a gasp of shock. All they could do was watch in horror as the scene played out.

What kind of a sick joke is this? By whose authority is he being sacrificed? He has done nothing to deserve death. These things were screaming through Melanna's mind.

The Ancients placed Noctli on the sacrificial altar and bound him. He was so calm. His friends wondered why he didn't resist.

Zonya was among Melanna's friends, watching. She had such grief in her heart that it almost felt like physical pain. Her tears flowed uncontrollably. The new love that had bloomed between them would be snuffed out this day. She was helpless only to watch what enfolded here.

Noctli's sacrifice would protect his friends for now. Only until Zafrina decided it was time to spill more blood, to target whoever she saw as a threat.

In a commanding voice, the Dark One started reciting the sacrificial chant. Her servants repeated each phrase after her in unison. And then the chanting became quicker and heightened. It pulled the crowd in at the foot of the pyramid. The crowd waved their fists in the air to the rhythm of the chant, beckoning the goddess onward. Then Zafrina slowly raised an ornate obsidian knife above her head. She quickly plunged the knife into the Noctli's chest. She cut out his heart and held it up for all to see. She slashed his right wrist in order for his blood to drip into an urn. No one could see behind her mask how she licked her lips or how her fangs glistened in anticipation of what would come. With the climax of the ceremonial evening over, the crowd slowly dispersed.

Noctli's body, drained of blood, was taken to a holding chamber inside the pyramid and laid on the floor beside a handful of people that were tied and gagged. These unfortunate people wouldn't be missed in the city. The smell of sweet, fresh blood caused the throats of the Ancients and their evil queen to burn with thirst. The Ancients removed their masks, revealing pasty, luminous faces with fangs ready to strike. Their black, demonic stares fixed on the fearful pulses at the necks of the humans. The humans strained in vain against their bonds at the sight of the hungry vampires. Horrific fear was in the eyes of the captives as they awaited their fate. The Ancients circled their prey and attacked in unison. No one could hear the blood-curdling screams of the victims as the people of Coba continued to drink and party through the night. The Ancients and their queen were overtaken by their feeding frenzy. The humans stopped thrashing about as they finally lay still and dead. Not a drop of blood was wasted.

Later in the royal palace, Melanna searched for her father, King Tetaneeka Achcauhtli. She was the younger of two daughters to the king. It was evident that she inherited her mother's beauty and grace. Jet-black, wavy hair fell in long cascades about her face and shoulders. Her ebony eyes were in a flawless face with a complexion that hinted of a perpetual youthful blush. Her gold embroidered robe and long dark hair flowed behind her as she stepped quickly through the palace, inquiring about her father's whereabouts. The king stood silently in the great courtyard, surrounded by lush tropical gardens. He was starring at the stars that twinkled in the early evening hours while his fingers were nervously fidgeting with his skinny beard. He stood there in his fine robes like a fat cat who has discovered a larger predator threatens him. She approached slowly and stood at his side.

The king acknowledged the presence of his daughter with a nod as he asked, "What can I do for you my daughter?" He then returned his attention to the twinkling stars and continued to squelch his fears.

Melanna's eyes were cast down as she said, "Father, why do you let this continue? All this senseless human sacrifice?"

And then her eyes met his. Her face was forlorn, eyebrows pinched, her face tear stained.

"Nocli was a friend of mine. He did nothing to deserve dying tonight. That could've been any of my other friends or even me! Don't you care about your people anymore?" Still waiting for a response, she said, "It didn't use to be this way in our worship of the gods. We have always been peaceful people, but...this," her voice was lost in sobs. Her lungs heaved with grief and she buried her face against her father's chest.

The king put on a stiff upper lip as he said, "First of all, daughter, it will never be you who will be sacrificed. None of my household will! I'll see to that! Secondly, there are some things that you don't understand right now," the king said with a wave of his hand as if he would like to dismiss the subject.

Tetaneeka couldn't deal with this outburst of female emotion, not while he had his own fears to deal with. He placed his hands on her shoulders and held her away from him to hold her gaze as he continued speaking.

"I am King, yes, but only in title. It is the Dark One that holds the real Power. The power of freedom or enslavement, of life or death. I am just a puppet in her hands! Her will is my bidding," he said with a shrug of his shoulders.

The king's eyes looked troubled at having to admit this to his daughter. But in the dark corners of the king's heart where no light had shined for years, it troubled him to see his daughter so distraught. He was not use to discussing such matters with her. But she was nearly grown up now, wise for her age of 19 years, and looked more like her mother every day. He continued to explain to her that not only were his hands tied, but also the people's hearts had changed ever since the coming of Zafrina and her Ancients. The people were use to the blood lust. They allowed themselves to be ruled by their fear and superstition.

"Father, your army is loyal to you as are your people. They will fight for you! They will help you to take control of the kingdom again!"

"You don't know what you speak of. You don't know these people. They are not human like you and I. Even though they are small in number, they are a powerful force to reckon with. Their Power is not of this world."

His voice trailed off as he said the last sentence, his eyes wide with fright. He tried not to let her see his trembling hands as he folded his arms across his chest, an effort to hold himself together. His eyes returned to the starry host of the night sky.

"Then what are we to do?" She said looking down again. Her eyes started to mist.

Tetaneeka wrung his hands as he passively said, "We can only hope in the coming of a New Age that Zafrina has promised. Only those who believe will be worthy to enter into this New Age. We need to be obedient and accept our fate."

Melanna's eyebrows pinched together but this time not from grief, but in anger.

"It would seem that she has you under her spell too. These are all lies! These self-proclaimed gods cannot be trusted with the fate of our people. None of us is safe! How many more will die? People that look to you for protection! These are your people! I will not accept this." She paused and flexed her jaw muscle. "I will always remember who I am. I would rather die than to be enslaved by those freaks that everyone is bowing to!" she said with her teeth clenched and tears welling up in her eyes.

Where was his compassion and courage? Were they dead like Noctli? Melanna turned and walked back into the palace, still dejected and without the answers that she wanted to hear from her father.

Neither the king nor the princess was aware that there was a spy hiding behind a pillar there in the great courtyard. A spy who would report these things to Zafrina. He made his way back to the pyramid and entered into the chamber of his queen.

Zafrina's chamber was filled with all sorts of silks, tapestries, gold trays, gold goblets, Mayan art sculptures, souvenirs of conquered civilizations, and gifts from centuries of adoring slaves. She was reclining on a luxurious bed, her ebony hair fanned out over the red silk covering. Her features were exotic and tempting, the tools she used to draw in her prey. She had almond shaped eyes set in an oval face with prominent cheek bones. Her lips were voluptuous and the color of cherries. One would never guess that she was over one thousand years old.

Her spy told her about the meeting between the king and his daughter just moments ago. The Dark One's eyes narrowed and her full lips became a thin line. Her body quivered with rage. And then her lips curled back to show glistening fangs.

She hissed, "It seems that the princess is becoming a problem. I'll have to deal with her later. The king cannot be dissuaded by his own daughter. I'll have to see to that personally."

2. THE GOLDEN AGE

For everything there is a season, and a time for every matter or purpose under heaven: a time to be born, and a time to die. Eccl. 3:1&2

Flash back to what seemed like a lifetime ago in the early reign of King Tetaneeka Achcauhtli. Times were not always so grim. The high point of his reign was when Tetaneeka was married to his lovely Mayan queen, Almika. Her name meant "she of the sun". Like the brilliance of the sun, Almika's beauty was unmatched in the kingdom. He worshipped the very ground that she walked on. If there was a heaven, this had to be it, the king thought. Their love inspired poets and songwriters throughout the Mayan world – and a vast world that was! The gods blessed the royal couple with the coming of their first child. They named their first daughter Eleuia which means "wish". Two years passed and the king and queen waited for the coming of their second child.

The second pregnancy didn't go well with Queen Almika. Every day was a physical challenge for the queen as she came into her ninth month of pregnancy. As fate would have it, an invitation came to Tetaneeka for the king and his queen to make an appearance at court in the Mayan kingdom of Chichen Itza. Tetaneeka asked Almika not to make the trip, but she was a dutiful wife. Her place was by his side. When they arrived at Chichen Itza, Queen Almika spent a sleepless night in great pain. She wandered outside of the castle toward the Sacred Sacrificial Cenote. It was a quarter of a mile from the castle.

These cenotes where formed in the limestone over thousands of years in various places of the Yucatan. They are very deep craters filled with fresh water. Some were used for consumption while others were used in sacrificing.

When Almika arrived there, she sat under a huge old tree that grew at the cenote's edge. Almika sent up earnest prayers to the gods to spare her life and the life of her unborn child. In between her chanting, she pulled a heavy gold ring from her finger and tossed it into the cenote as a gift to the gods. She rocked back and forth and continued to pray.

Her maidservants, noticing her absence, scrambled to look for her. When they found her, it was too late to move her. The baby was coming. They cleared the ground as best they could. They also administered a special brew that would speed up the labor. Using the trunk of the tree for support, Almika bit down on a soft branch when a huge labor pain swept over her. This was taking too long. Something was wrong, and Almika was growing weaker. Finally, after what seemed like an eternity, a little head popped out. Her maidservants helped pull the rest of the baby out. There was so much blood that followed. Queen Almika continued to worsen as her life's blood left her body. Almika's maidservants took the infant back to the castle and tried to round up some strong men to carry the queen back into the castle.

Suddenly, Almika found herself looking up into the face of a beautiful stranger who stood above her, mesmerized at the scene he'd just witnessed. Actually, it was the salty, sweet smell of her blood that caught his attention even though he was several miles away. The queen felt an odd sense of comfort lying beside this man that she didn't know. The stranger dropped to one knee and held her eyes with his own dark ones. In those dark eyes one could see power as well as compassion. Her beauty was not lost on him, but in fact, reminded him of someone very dear to him in the past. It stirred his blood inside of him. Almika raised her hand to take hold of his and tried to make the most of the final moments of her life.

The stranger cradled the queen's head as she spoke to him in a low voice.

"I don't know who you are, but I feel that I can trust you. Please promise me that you will protect my baby, if it is within your power to do so. I know that the gods will reward you in your efforts to do this. And I'll be eternally grateful."

The stranger looked deep into her eyes and for a brief moment, her pain became his own as flashes of the past flickered in his mind. His eyes were kind and warm. Were those tears that welled up in his eyes? He nodded slowly to the queen that he could be entrusted with this promise.

Almika gave him a faint smile and her eyes fluttered and closed. The stranger laid her head gently back to the ground. He went back to his hiding place at the jungle's edge just as the king along with a group of burly men came to carry the queen into the castle. Almika had almost no pulse as Teteneeka arrived next to his wife's side. He took her hand and looked into her face. She opened her eyes and smiled the best she could.

"Everything will be all right, my love," assured Teteneeka.

With her hand raised to his cheek, she said, "I'm sorry. I hope I didn't disappoint you. I know you wanted a son so badly."

"You could never disappoint me! Never! All I want is you! You are my rising sun and my beautiful moon. We will get you back to the castle. You'll be up on your feet in no time," as he managed a smile.

"No, my King. I'm afraid I *will* have to disappoint you. I feel my body getting colder and my life slipping away. Please... love *both* of our daughters and take care of them, my lovvv..."

And with that, her hand fell from his face and the queen breathed her last breath. The men lifted the still body of the queen and carried her into the castle where everyone was in shock and in mourning at these turn of events.

The dark stranger came out of the jungle again to look for the gold ring that he had seen Almika throw into the cenote. The queen had charged him as a protector to her daughter. So the ring may come in handy one day. He saw a glint of gold shine on top of some debris next to a skull. It was an easy descent for him, but reaching it was a whole different story. With the help of a leg bone, he was able to pull the pile closer until he could grab the ring. Once the ring was in his possession, he climbed back up to the top and once again melted into the jungle.

They bore Almika's body back to Coba for burial. The entire kingdom turned out for the funeral, as she was much loved among the people. A grand procession of musicians followed the queen's casket. When the casket was laid in the ground, the musicians broke their instruments, and tossed them into the grave as a last sacrifice to their beloved queen. People brought gifts of exotic flowers, fruits and trinkets that they left at the burial site. Tetaneeka was touched by the outpouring of love and grief of his people. But his heart was now an empty shell. On the inside he felt numb and cold as ice.

After the death of Queen Almika, Tetaneeka's world fell apart with the loss of his love. For many months, he could not bring himself to touch the one responsible for his true love's death which he attributed to the birth of his daughter. Baby Melanna was left exclusively in the care of her nannies most of the time. Tetaneeka only inquired about her every now and then. Deep in his heart he never forgave his child for sending his true love to her grave.

As the years went by after the queen's death, Tetaneeka dedicated most of his time to acquiring more power and ruling his people. He tried to spend the least amount of time with his own children. He was a stranger in his own palace. If his daughters needed immediate attention, he had little patience for that. A nanny was called promptly. To him, his children were like annoying little gnats to be shooed away. He grew more distant and slovenly as the years went by. His only saving grace was that he had loyal servants who kept him and the palace together.

The king was never able to give Melanna his whole heart, as a father should, but instead, treated her with coolness in the line of duty. Melanna never had a deep relationship with her father and never knew the love of a mother. Yet, all of her needs were met materially. She never wanted for anything. But there remained a large hole in her heart that should have been filled by loving parents. Melanna grew to be a lovely young woman with a gracious and friendly personality. Her father had to admit to himself that he had pride in his daughter for the beautiful woman she had become.

During these years, the people of Tetaneeka's kingdom knew prosperity and happiness. One was free to worship the god of his choosing and participate in Mayan religious traditions that were passed down from generation to generation. Coba became the largest Mayan city of Southeastern Mexico and in the Yucatan and served as a hub of trade to these regions. Coba became a thriving, multicultural city that had influences from Mayan, Caribbean, Mexican, and Spanish cultures. Teteneeka did so well in the growth and development of Coba that his influence grew throughout the Mayan nations.

In the city of Coba as Melanna grew up, Tetaneeka provided the finest tutors for her education. His only desire was to see that she was properly schooled and dressed in order that she wouldn't be an embarrassment to the palace.

Melanna insisted on finishing her last couple of school years with the other children her age. She wanted so much to fit in and experience everything there was in a public school. When she wasn't studying, all her time was spent shopping at the street vendors, partying, and vying for the affections of the most handsome young men. She had a small group of close-knit friends that she constantly hung out with. These friends, Teela, Zonya and Nelli, she considered her extended family. They were close enough to be considered sisters without actually being related. They did everything together and shared secrets. She could tell her friends things that she couldn't tell her own father, the one who ruled the kingdom. Her friends most likely knew her better than her own father as sad as this fact was, but true none the less. So Melanna and her friends planned an afternoon of shopping. No servants, nannies, or politicians would be along for the trip. It was time to enjoy life and be with the ones who cared about you the most.

3. GIRLS JUST WANNA HAVE FUN

…A time to keep, and a time to cast away. Eccl. 1:6

Melanna and her friends took off for the market place in the late morning. The humidity was down a bit, which was a rare thing living so close to the rain forests. She could tell that they were going to have a good time today. The weather was almost perfect. They walked along the streets of Coba as they gossiped. Their skirts and their long dark hair blew in the gentle tropical breeze.

The Mayan people participated in trade with countries that lined the shores of the Gulf of Mexico as well as the Caribbean Islands. People traded in seashells, obsidian, salt, jade, fine fabrics, spices, and perfumes. The street was alive with people trying to get good bargains. There were a lot of things to see: bushels of fresh flowers, woven artistry made from reeds that swayed in the wind, cages of chickens, crates of vegetables, spices and so much more. Finally they came to vendors who sold seashell jewelry and other accessories. Melanna was enthralled. She wasn't leaving until she bought something here. But her friends managed to pull her away and to convince her to watch the entertainment. The merchandise wasn't going anywhere.

They stood and watched young peasant women dancing to the music of a tortoise shell, maracas, wooden flute, and small drums. The women performed a dance that was handed down through the generations. They lifted their left arms gracefully over their heads while their right hands held the hem of their colorful, woven skirts. It was a blur of pink, purple, red, blue, and green as they twirled to the music. It was like watching an early form of primal ballet, only with more passion and sensuality. When the dance ended, people threw money at the dancers' feet. The women bowed graciously.

As Melanna and her three friends walked through the market place, they came to a vendor that was selling fabrics. Melanna pulled a berry colored woven fabric from the vendor's table and draped the front of herself with it.

Zonya, who spent more time outdoors under the Mayan sun than her friends, brushed her sun-streaked hair from her face said, "You would really look pretty in a dress made from that material. Not like the same ol' boring woven dresses that everyone wears with patterns that are passed down from one generation to the next."

Melanna wondered out loud, "Do you really think it would compliment me?"

"Absolutely! And you could wear it to the Bonfire Night that's scheduled before the end of the school year."

Teela, the shortest one in their group and with dimpled cheeks, piped up, "Yes! It would drive Manny crazy to see you looking so tempting and delicious!" She made a sound like a jungle cat and clawed the air for emphasis, which brought a flurry of giggles from all of them. Melanna smiled in amusement as she shook her head at her friend's teasing.

"Oh, stop it, you guys. You know better than that! I've known Manny all my life. He is nothing more than a close friend. I'm pretty sure he feels the same way."

She still clung to the fabric and posed from side to side, causing her long, jet-black, wavy hair to bounce with her movements. Her body was shapely and feminine, but not too petite.

Nelli crossed her arms across her chest as she took in the sight of her friend. Of the four young women, Nelli was the most mature one in looks and in disposition. She had a tan oval-shaped face with inquisitive eyes that always studied everything around her.

"He's a guy, isn't he? He'll look at you differently if you're wearing a dress made from that!" Nelli was always the most transparent of all of them. She always said things from the heart, not withholding anything. She lived up to the meaning of her name which means "truth".

"Or not wearing one!" said Teela.

Teela immediately ducked to avoid Melanna's flailing fists. The girls burst out into laughter. She continued to speak from the safety of a table between them.

"I would wager that he would even make some moves on you too. At least a kiss."

More giggles came from the group with that remark.

"Ya, what's wrong with a kiss or two?" asked Nelli. "Otherwise, it would truly be boring!"

"You just tend to your own affairs with Yoltzin. He's got the hots for you, doesn't he? The bonfire won't be the only thing that will be burning that night!" teased Melanna.

"That's right. I'm working out a plan. I know of a secret spot to take Yoltzin to where we could spend some romantic time all alone," said Nelli.

"You'll be caught and forced to spend the rest of the celebration under the watchful eye of the elders," Zonya cut in. "Don't do anything stupid to jeopardize the ceremony. It wouldn't look good for you, seeing that you do have to make a speech and all."

"I suppose you're right," Nelli said with a mock pucker to her lip. "I'll just have to sneak some stolen moments when no one is looking to work my magic," she added with a mischievous grin.

Melanna paid the vendor for the fabric, and the girls continued shopping. They lingered at a little shop that sold exotic perfumes and bath oils. Melanna had her eye on an ornate, vase-like bottle of perfume. She always had an eye for the expensive stuff. It was the best smelling fragrance that she had ever experienced. This perfume along with a gorgeous berry colored dress would be perfect for Bonfire Night. Nelli chose to buy some imported bath oil. Teela and Zonya sampled fragrances here and there but ultimately just wanted to continue shopping. Neither of them had boyfriends at this time, and, therefore, didn't feel the need to impress anybody with fragrance or a new dress.

While the girls still lingered at the perfume vendor's shop, Eleuia appeared on the arm of a young man who Melanna recognized as a palace guard named Mulac. Eleuia was so engrossed in the products that she didn't see Melanna right away.

Melanna was fully aware when her sister entered the shop although she didn't greet her, and for good reason. She avoided her at every cost. It was as though Eleuia's purpose in life was to spew bitterness toward her sister. In fact she delighted in making Melanna's life a living hell. She decided instead to pay the vendor for the perfume and make a retreat. After searching for the money in her satchel, she realized that she didn't have enough.

Melanna looked thoroughly embarrassed as she said to the shop owner, "I'm so sorry. I'm short of money after my last purchase. I'll have to come back with more money to buy this."

Eleuia walked up to Melanna and said, "By the gods! What are *you* doing here? Aren't you out of your element?"

Melanna rolled her eyes and responded, "Why don't you take your fan club and just leave."

"And not fulfill one of my missions in life: to enjoy making my little sister miserable? I wouldn't think of it."

"I wish you would grow up and just leave me alone."

"I heard they were interviewing for pig farmers. You can make it if you hurry," Eleuia said with a scathing tone.

Mulac gave her a squeeze around the waist and kissed the top of her head. He took pleasure in the way Eleuia degraded her sister.

"And are you in town for the Witches' Ball? Just do us all a favor. Get on your broom and fly out of here!" Melanna shot back.

Melanna turned to exit with her friends, but she hesitated, seeing Eleuia approach the shop owner. Eleuia picked up the bottle, savored the fragrance, and laid her payment of coins on the table.

"I'd like to pay for this."

"Ah, that's nice of you to buy this for your sister."

"Oh, it's not for her. I intend to use it myself."

The shop owner gave her a disbelieving look but was happy to take her money. But before the transaction was complete, Eleuia *accidently* knocked the bottle to the ground. It shattered filling the whole place with a heavy perfume scent. And she was not about to part with her money.

"Oops!" Eleuia put her hands to her lips mockingly.

She and Mulac strolled out of the shop arm in arm while her laughter trailed behind her.

It pained Melanna that her sister treated her with such disdain as she had at that moment. What had she done to deserve it?

The girls watched the retreating backs of the couple as they went into the market place and melted into the crowd.

"I'm sorry, sir. I'll bring you the money and pay for this. I promise."

"It wasn't your fault," the shop owner said with kind eyes. "I'll send the bill to the palace. I'm sure your father, the king, is good for it."

Once they were out of the shop and out of hearing, Nelli broke the silence.

"Why do you let her treat you that way?" she asked as she came close to hug her friend.

Melanna shrugged, "That's okay. I really didn't need it anyway. Let's not dwell on it. Let's just try to enjoy ourselves."

"I agree," said Zonya, "It's not worth our time to let someone like that spoil our day for us."

The girls continued on into the market. They just wanted to have fun. After all, this was the time for bonding with your friends and making memories. It was as if they knew they were nearing the cross roads of their lives. They would soon be making choices that would change their lives forever. It was time to savor these moments.

There was a small group of boys from school who had been watching Melanna and her friends as they shopped. They gave the girls bold stares as they made comments to each other amongst themselves. The girls finally wised up to the attention they were receiving. So the girls pretended not to notice the boys, but instead decided to have a little fun.

Zonya pretended *accidentally* to drop a piece of clothing on the ground. She slowly bent over to retrieve it, looking provocative as she did so, caressing her legs and her butt. The boys' eyes narrowed and their lips puckered with a look of "How sweet!"

Teela took an orange slice from her cool, tropical drink, tilted her head back, and slid it over her throat and down her chest. She then brought it up between her lips to suck on. This brought verbal moans from the group of boys.

Nelli stood facing the boys and held up a tiny piece of clothing over her breasts that looked as if it were meant for a honeymoon. Her eyes went from the garment to the boys. She blew them a kiss.

And then the boys knew that they had been played. The girls broke out in laughter. The boys, with their egos intact, decided peruse the market place for other unsuspecting girls to peep at.

The girls spotted a food vendor selling tortillas and beans under a tiny thatched hut. They wolfed down some food before heading back home.

Once home, Melanna made her way through the palace to her bedroom where she unloaded her purchases of the day. She thought a swim would be nice. After she wrapped her body in a covering that was embellished with embroidery and beads, she headed toward the courtyard. Melanna's bare feet made no sound as she stopped behind the door that stood slightly ajar, of the Great Room where her father discussed the affairs of his people with his closest advisors. The topic was the food trade with the surrounding nations and storage of their harvests.

By the gods! How boring!

She slipped by unnoticed into the courtyard. This tropical garden always helped her to put her life into balance. She approached the pool that reflected the sky above. The water was undisturbed and gave the appearance of glass. There appeared to be no one else in the courtyard. Melanna untied her covering, let it fall to the floor, and entered the water naked. The dust and her weariness soon disappeared. She closed her eyes and listened to the sounds around her: the breeze blowing in from above, the palm fronds and tropical plants rustling in the breeze, and the sounds of children playing outside the palace. Melanna made several laps back and forth under and above the water. Then she floated on her back, gliding slowly as she looked up at the lazy sky. She closed her eyes for a brief moment.

And then there came a faint whisper on the breeze.

"Melanna. Beautiful Melanna."

She opened her eyes and looked around in every direction. Was it her imagination? Was someone watching her? She suddenly felt exposed and vulnerable.

"Hello? Is someone there?" she asked, trying to hide her fear.

She tried to cover her breasts with her arms. There was no answer. Her eyes darted all around trying to locate any movement. She wondered if one of the servants was invading her privacy. Finally her eyes rested on a lilac-crowned Amazon parrot that was looking at her from a perch under a palm. It spread its brilliant green wings in a lazy stretch as it mumbled something inaudible. Melanna, now covered with goose bumps, shivered as she stepped out of the pool and covered herself with her wrap. She walked off in the direction of her bedroom. When she had gone, a tall male figure stepped out from among the shadows. He wore a silver talisman inlaid with turquoise and orange argillite that glittered in the filtered light on this chest. His dark eyes were full of desire as well as protectiveness. His hair was as dark as a raven, wavy, and short at the nape of his neck. The shadows of the palm fronds danced over his smooth, bare, chest that rippled with muscles.

"Thanks for covering for me," he said to the bird.

The bird in response bobbed up and down as if to say, "No problem," followed by a shrill wolf whistle.

"Yes, my thoughts exactly!"

The man pondered for a short moment with a pleased look on this face and then slipped silently out of the palace, unnoticed.

The next day, Melanna took her new fabric to her personal servant, Qaileen. Qaileen was the most important person in the palace to Melanna, second only to her father the king. Melanna hardly thought of her as a servant, but as a family member. She was everything to Melanna: seamstress, advisor, surrogate parent, a shoulder to cry on, and much more. The feelings between them were mutual. Qaileen thought of Melanna as her own daughter. She filled a gap in Melanna's heart that needed to be filled. A gap created by the loss of a mother and the negligence of a father.

Melanna laid the fabric in Qaileen's arms with simple instructions adding, "You know what I like. I trust you," she said with an impish grin.

Qaileen knew that Melanna was interested in a style that would show off a little cleavage and hug her figure. A style that would present her best assets and would still leave something to the imagination.

Out of curiosity Melanna asked, "Qaileen, was there a servant working in the courtyard yesterday afternoon after I returned from shopping?"

"No, little one. All of them retired to their quarters for the evening except for me and the cook. And he was too busy fixing a feast for the advisors that your father had in the Great Room."

Melanna ventured into the courtyard where she encountered one of the gardeners who was standing near the Amazon parrot. He was admiring a bougainvillea that had refused to bloom under his care until now. It was as if a miracle had occurred. Not only was it blooming large purple blooms, but it had grown fifteen feet over night, twining around neighboring palm trees. It also draped over the pot and covered the floor at the base in a carpet of purple. Melanna knew that this flowering vine was not like this when she swam here the night before. Yet she had no explanation for it now. She also stood in awe of the beautiful bougainvillea.

"Sir, were you or one of the other gardeners here in the late afternoon or evening hours?"

"No, child. None of us were scheduled to work yesterday. Why?"

"It's nothing. And by the way, you did a great job with this flowering shrub."

"I can't take credit for it. It was dying under my care. But a strange miracle happened. It just had a giant spurt of growth and is now covered in flowers. It looked small and withered just a day or two ago," he shrugged. "But, again, back to your question. No one was here in the courtyard yesterday, princess."

Melanna seemed satisfied with that answer for the moment. Maybe her imagination got away from her yesterday. She decided to dismiss any further investigation, for now anyway.

Little did they know that the miracle of the bougainvillea had occurred when the uninvited stranger had hidden next it in the courtyard. His heart was filled with such desire, that Power flowed through him, causing the bougainvillea to come to life. As an immortal, the ability to effect plant life was one of his gifts.

The anticipation grew as Melanna looked forward to the coming festivities. Her heart was filled with hopes and dreams; her life was a book with blank pages for her to write.

4. WOMEN'S RITE OF PASSAGE

Before the festivities for the end of the school year were held, the pilgrimage of the Women's Rite of Passage was to take place for all young women who had come of age. Young women from all over the Yucatan traveled to Isla Cozumel to honor the Mayan goddess IxChel, the goddess of love and fertility. The island was located on the North Eastern coast of the Yucatan, just thirty-seven miles south of Cancun. The girls from Coba were excited to go on this trip as was Melanna. It was a milestone that officially ushered girls into womanhood. The trip was an enjoyable one with lots of talking amongst many groups of girls along the way. Some of the topics were about wedding plans for those who were betrothed already. Others were about how they would miss school or not miss it after it was over. Melanna mostly listened to what others had to say, only joining in the laughter.

The girls were treated to glimpses of the wildlife along the way, such as the many spider monkeys and parrots in the trees above, and the occasional iguana sunbathing on a tree limb or rock. A small group of pig-like tapirs were seen foraging for leaves and tender shoots. And also a jaguar gave some girls a scare as he peeked through the jungle leaves at them; their screams sent him flying in the opposite direction through the jungle. Immediately afterward the girls laughed at themselves.

When the long procession arrived at the coast, there were men who were assigned the task of ferrying the young women to the island. How exciting! It was like a mini-adventure.

Upon arrival to the island, Priestess Cualli greeted the young women and escorted them to their thatched huts they would be staying in for the duration of the pilgrimage. The huts were located on the beach as was the temple of the goddess IxChel.

Once everyone had arrived, the girls gathered around Priestess Cualli for introductions. She called out the names of the cities of the Yucatan, and each group of girls raised their hands as their city was called out. All were present that were invited. The priestess then began her talk about how she came to be the priestess on Isla Cozumel, the history of this pilgrimage, and the importance of the pilgrimage to all Mayan women. This blessing would ensure the survival of the Mayan people. The introduction took them into the evening hours. The priestess dismissed the girls by saying that they would continue in the morning.

The girls settled in their places on the floors of the huts. Chattering could be heard well into the night.

The next morning as the sun arose, schools of small fish could be seen jumping through the surf with larger predator fish chasing after them. The brown pelicans and seagulls also tried to feed on the small fish as they were driven to the surface. Songbirds filled the salty air with their singing from the tops of trees that stood away from the beach. Orange wildflowers grew in grassy clumps near the shoreline. The hum of nature permeated the air and heightened the senses of the visiting young women.

It is said that the water is so clear that if one holds his breath long enough, he can swim to a place under water that has ancient statues and pieces of broken pillars. One can even see groups of star fish on the sandy bottom too. Isla Cozumel was home to beautiful reefs. The creatures in the sea were just as beautiful as the ones that inhabited the island if not more so.

After the young women had breakfast, they prepared themselves with the appropriate attire to enter the Temple of IxChel.

The young women spent much time in talk, meditation and prayer. Priestess Cualli wrote out a contract of sorts that all Mayan women would uphold from that day forward: honoring her husband; giving herself freely to her husband in order to have children; and honoring the gods in all they do. The last of the ritual concluded with a small blood sacrifice in which each girl made a small cut on her own finger. The blood from the cut was then smeared directly on the idol that represented the goddess IxChel. Blood was also smeared on the document with the written contract. After the collection of the blood, the document was then thrown into the fire, sealing the promise of all who "signed" it.

One last blessing was pronounced over the young women, and then they filtered out of the temple, eager to spend time on the island before heading back home.

Melanna and her three friends changed into something more beach-appropriate. They tried using their shawls to gather their skirts up to avoid getting them wet in the surf as they walked. They strolled down the beach until they spied a shack with fresh fish. The owner was pleased to serve some tourists. The girls were seated on some rough planks at a rickety table. The "Catch of the Day" seemed to be a popular pick for all of them.

After they gave their orders to the owner, they waited patiently for their food to arrive at their table. They occupied themselves with watching the surf and the sandpipers running to and fro at a comical pace to beat the foamy waves as they looked for food.

Zonya and Nelli talked about the highlights of Priestess Cualli's teachings. Teela giggled and stared at a young local boy who was winking at her from his seat behind them. He continued doing so just to see her dimpled smile. The local boys certainly had many females to ogle over as small groups of girls paraded up and down the beach.

But one local in particular caught Melanna's eye. She happened to be facing the ocean and saw a huge shark break the surface with a man grasping the dorsal fin, swimming alongside the big fish. There appeared to be a stream of blood flowing from beneath the man's face as if he had bitten the shark. Melanna's jaw dropped in wonder.

"Do I see what I think I'm seeing? Or does that fool have a death wish?" She turned to her friends and said, "Look at that guy! Have you ever seen anything like that? Could he be injured?"

Melanna got the attention of the owner as she pointed to the shark and the man swimming just beyond the surf. Then both were suddenly gone out of sight under the surface.

Excitedly she said, "I just saw the oddest thing! I saw a young man swimming with a shark. It looked like the man had-"

"Yes! That is one of the locals who enjoys showing off for the tourists! Don't worry. He never gets hurt doing his stunts."

The owner narrowed his eyes. He turned his back to the girls then he cringed and gnashed his teeth. He needed to guard a secret that he didn't want to be spread.

With a forced smile, he turned to the girls and said, "I've known him for a long time now. He loves the attention he gets from the pretty girls that visit."

"Really! What lengths that some guys will go to for attention these days!" Zonya said with disgust in her voice. She shielded her eyes from the sun as she watched for signs of him in the surf while the ocean breeze played with her sun streaked hair.

"Is it working?" Nelli asked while she leaned on her elbow and rested her petite oval shaped face in her hand. Melanna only smirked and rolled her eyes.

After eating some fish along with some fresh fruit, the girls decided to explore the island. They started walking south near the beach. They quickened their pace to catch up to a group of girls that were ahead of them.

Something caught Melanna's eye at the edge of a cenote near a group of trees that bent over to block partial view of it. It looked like a huge black shadow that went over the edge. Melanna told her friends that she would catch up to them.

She parted the trees and cautiously approached the giant pit. Melanna got on her knees at the edge and peered over. Thick vines tangled the walls. A glimmer of water could barely be seen from the sparse lighting. Little rocks tumbled over the edge making a splashing noise as they fell into the water below. To her utter horror, Melanna's hands came in contact with some slick rock and she started pitching forward, down, down into the cenote. She screamed as she helplessly veered toward her fateful end. It almost seemed like she was in slow motion. Was she imagining it or were the vines coming alive and aiding her in her plight? Her eyes grew wilder with fright and another horrific scream escaped her lips. The vines snaked out of the sides of the pit and coiled around her legs and waist.

This can't be happening!

It seemed like she fell forever until the impact of the water, but she was not completely submerged. That didn't entirely feel like water. Did she fall on a tree at the bottom? The cool, smooth tree was moving her through the water. Then Melanna's mind shut down as it retreated into the safety of blackness.

5. AN UNEXPECTED GUEST

Tez could sense the curious eyes of a human as she searched for signs of life at the bottom of his cenote. But he never in his wildest dreams thought that anyone would just drop in on him. As soon as he heard the scream, he moved with such speed that the human eye could not see him. He dove into the water under the human. He raised his arms and commanded the vines to do his bidding as they came alive, slowing her descent as they twined about her. He braced himself for the human bundle that tumbled in his arms. Even though there were no serious injuries, Melanna went into shock. She blacked out in his arms, with most of her body submerged in the water and her dark hair fanning out around her head on the surface. For a moment Tez took in the features of the innocent, beautiful face, so much like the face of her mother he looked into nineteen years ago before she died giving birth. This has truly come full circle for him. What were the odds of this happening? Tez tucked Melanna under his right arm and swam to the edge with his left one. After pulling her out of the water, he laid her still body on the rocks and accessed her injuries. Her hands and arms had gashes on them as she had tried in vain to find a stronghold to break the fall. The thirst immediately burned his throat. How long had it been since he was this close to a beautiful woman, to hear her heart beat pumping warm, sweet blood through her veins; to feel her soft skin and silky dark hair and smell her fragrance?

A moan escaped her lips waking him out of his musings. Her forehead was bruised and bloodied. He couldn't determine how bad this injury was. He lifted her shirt to see if anything was broken or bleeding there. Her side had lacerations along her rib cage. Tez immediately covered her with a blanket to keep her warm. He found some herbs that he could apply to her wounds to help her heal. And then he waited in the shadows.

Melanna eventually came around. Her hand immediately found the injury on her forehead as she dabbed it with her fingers. She winced. A few drops of blood were on her fingertips.

The man who was concealed in shadows not far from where she lay asked, "How are you feeling?"

"I seem to hurt everywhere at the moment, but I'm sure I'll be fine."

"You mind telling me what were you doing? You know you could've easily been killed!" he said as if reprimanding a child.

Melanna shook her head slightly to clear it and tried to focus on her surroundings. She looked around cautiously before answering.

"I saw something strange go over the edge of the cenote. It didn't look like an animal or a person. My curiosity got the better of me. But don't worry. I'll be out of your hair soon enough."

She hugged her arms around her body for warmth and security.

"My friends don't know that I'm here."

With that admission, fear started to creep up her spine. She shook it off and tried to get up. She felt a little woozy and decided to wait a few more minutes.

Tez could sense her rapid pulse and read her emotions easily. She had a unique smell to him, like musky wildflowers. Her emotions only heightened it.

"You have nothing to fear of me. I don't usually ensnare young women to fall into this place."

He was unable to make her smile. He stood looking down at her with his arms folded across his chest. He tried a different approach.

"My only concern right now is to see that you are well enough to return to your girl friends on the beach. I've tried to treat your injuries the best that I can."

He came into the filtered light and knelt down on the floor of the cave. Her eyes locked with his dark ones like a frightened deer. She sensed that he spoke the truth. Maybe she could trust him. She didn't have much choice in the matter. He wore only a dark blue pair of woven pants that were rolled up below the knees and a silver talisman made with turquoise and orange argillite that dangled from a chain on his well-muscled chest. The talisman that he wore protected him from turning to a heap of ash in the sunlight, a curse to all immortals. She had never seen such beauty in a man in all her life. His muscular build made him look better equipped than the finest soldier in her father's army. Water beaded over his bronze skin in the dim light. His hair was in wet ringlets. It was as if she had just met her own personal angel, a gift from the gods. He looked a lot like the young man she had seen swimming with the shark. She wanted to ask him about it, but since it seemed so farfetched, she didn't bother. Instead, she turned her attention to her own appearance. She must have looked a terrible sight after having been fished out of the water in a disheveled heap. She now felt embarrassed at being seen like this by such a handsome man. The blood rose to her cheeks. She pulled her shirt up to expose the raw looking ribs. The healing herb leaves still clung to her skin. Then she looked down at herself and realized that her clothing was torn in several places. Well, at least all the important parts were covered up.

"I don't remember seeing you on the beach. How do you know that I was with my friends?" She eyed him cautiously.

"It *is* a special religious Rite of Passage, is it not? Besides, I was enjoying a swim. And I always notice pretty girls when they come to visit the island."

After having said that, it was as if his eyes had taken the scenic route on her body until they reached her face again.

Melanna could feel her face feeling hot under his gaze. No doubt she was an even brighter shade of red than before. But she couldn't pass up the opportunity now that he had brought up the subject.

"So that *was you* swimming with a shark just now? Uh, do you do that often?"

The stranger looked at her, deep in thought before answering.

His eyes seemed to soften as he said, "Sorry for being rude." He extended his hand to gently and briefly clasp Melanna's hand in welcome. "My name is Tezcatli Uetzcayotl. But people call me Tez. Yes, you could say that it's a hobby of mine. It makes the tourists happy. They spend money and that makes the vendors happy. And then I get free drinks, so it makes me happy."

A brilliant smile followed his last remark, but his eyes didn't mirror the smile for they hid the untold truth. He poured some cool water into a cup and offered it to her which she gladly took. Her eyes drank in his beauty and quenched her in ways that the water never could. His voice was comforting, drawing her in.

"This happens to be a home away from home, a place that I stay at when I'm visiting the island."

She watched him pour a drink for himself of what appeared to be red wine.

"The natives of the past made these caves down here in order to be able to escape the sweltering heat. I find it rather comfortable. Nobody bothers me down here. That is...except for you."

And with that, he flashed a beautiful, devilish smile at her that both disarmed her and made her discomfited. This time his eyes smiled too. Her lips parted as she involuntarily exhaled.

"Now tell me who you are and what brings you to my humble abode."

Melanna thought it wise not to tell Tez that she was Teteneeka's daughter. So she stated the facts apart from that truth.

"I'm Melanna Coszcatl. And, yes, I came with a group of young women from Coba to participate in the Right of Passage ceremony." Melanna clutched the blanket to herself for warmth and continued to look at her surroundings. "Since it's over, we will probably be heading back pretty soon. I hope that my friends are not worried about me."

She hoped he would take the hint and help her get to the surface on the beach. He ignored the hint and continued his charade. He needed to be more convincing that she could trust him. He would win her over if it were the last thing he did today.

"Hmmm. I think I remember seeing you around Coba." He pretended to search his memory as he squinted his eyes and grabbed his chin. "Yes! You are Teteneeka's daughter, aren't you? That's right! I believe I'm acquainted with your sister, Eleuia."

Melanna arched one eyebrow and asked, "How so?"

"One evening I was having a drink with some local boys. How many rounds did we have? I can't remember. But we had some girls with us to keep us amused. Eleuia happened to be one of them." Peeping at her out of the corner of his eye, he was pleased that at the mention of Eleuia, she made a horrible face. He continued, "I decided that she just wasn't my type. I hope that you don't mind me saying..."

"No! Please, do go on. You were saying?"

"She's too much into herself. She's rebellious, spoiled and just plain wicked!" He put on a sour face as he made his assessment and tried to be convincing that these traits were beneath him. He turned his face away, but he looked at Melanna out of the corner of his eye for her reaction.

"Wow," she said in mock disbelief, "All that from one night out with the boys with some 'distractions'?" A crooked smile crept over her face. "I'm afraid that you're very observant though. My sister is exactly how you've described her. She and I are like night and day. Sometimes I wonder if we are really related. But I'm reminded everyday that I killed our mother when she gave birth to me. Eleuia does not let me forget that fact."

This revelation got Tez's hackles up as he said, "Don't be ridiculous! You had no say about coming into this world or to what family you would belong to. Your sister is seething with bitterness. People like that delight in making other people miserable just as she is making you."

Tez had to be careful not to reveal that he knew more about her life than what he was letting on. He came closer to Melanna, close enough to touch her and went on. He held her attention with his dark eyes, and she was falling into the depths of them.

"I believe that everyone is born with a purpose. Each of us has to find what that purpose is." He let that truth sink in before he went on. "You must believe that your mother loved you very much even if she did not survive to tell you." He dare not say any more on the subject. At least for now anyway.

Melanna, still curious, asked, "What about your family? Where are they?"

"I have no family." He looked down at the floor of the cave as he was filled with sadness at this admission. "I am the last of my kinsmen. I had a wife many years ago. She now walks the spirit world. When she died, part of me died with her. I've never been the same since."

" 'Many years ago'? You make it sound like you're an old man. You look to be about 25 years old."

Tez turned to look into her eyes. His face showed no emotion, yet his emotions ran deep about who he was, where he came from, and the struggle of accepting what he had become. If she only knew that inside he was a very old man, but he was locked forever in his unchanging body. The body of a vampire protected from the sun by the talisman that he wore around his neck. He was always trying to hang on to a tiny shred of his past humanity. Always fighting with the thirst that threatened to overpower him. The thirst for blood. Human blood was always the best, but Tez maintained a clear conscience in that he feasted on the blood of animals and big fish of the sea. The fact that Tez fed on animal and fish blood instead of human blood did not make him a weaker vampire. On the contrary, the larger and deadlier the animal or fish, the more Power Tez derived from it. That is why his blood of choice was from big sharks and jaguars.

Sitting in such close proximity to Melanna with her fresh wounds was more than he could bear. His face grew fiendishly dark with the thirst. At that moment, the monster inside of him wanted to spring on her and to feast on her sweet blood. She would not be able to stop him. No one would hear her cry for help. She was, after all, just a weak human, and a beautiful one at that. A gift from the gods lay at his feet. And no witnesses. He quickly got to his feet and retreated to the shadows once more. He turned his face away from her as he shut his eyes tightly and breathed deeply, struggling to get a handle on his craving. Melanna thought that she saw a change in Tez's expression, but it happened so fast that she dismissed it. Unaware of Tez's attempt at some distance, Melanna felt as though she could spend the rest of her day getting to know him better, even if it meant in a dimly lit cave.

Tez struggled for composure and he said with a ragged voice, "I think it's time that you return to your friends. They may be looking for you. We shouldn't worry them. And the last thing I want is for people to be snooping around here."

Melanna was disappointed at having the conversation cut short.

"Will I see you again? Will you be coming to Coba soon?"

"Sure I will. Will your father mind if I visit?"

"He really doesn't have to know. I'm always spending time with friends. It's not like he really ever notices that I'm not in the palace anyway." A brief moment of sadness swept over her at this admission. But she added, "Besides, I'm a young woman now and old enough to make my own choices."

Tez cocked his head at an angle and replied, "That sounded like it came from a strong, capable young woman of the world. Good for you!" His eyes thoughtfully lingered on her as they appraised her.

Tez took Melanna by the hand, which caused butterflies in her stomach. His hand was cool and strong yet gentle. He helped her to her feet, gazed into her face and said, "Do you feel well enough to walk?"

Almost breathless, she answered, "Yes, I think I'll be okay."

He led her through the dark corners of the cave and up some hidden steps to the surface above. She walked out of the tree line towards the beach. When she turned to address Tez, he was gone. Her eyes scanned the trees and in all directions before going on. She slowly made her way to the beach with her eyes dreamily on the crashing waves. Then to her surprise a dorsal fin of a shark appeared beyond the sandbar with Tez hitching a ride once more. With a swift backward motion of his head, he whipped his wet hair back from his eyes, and smiled at Melanna who stood there with her mouth open in awe. The surprised expression turned into a smile and she waved to him. Her heart pounded erratically. Both Tez and the big fish plunged under the surface in one fluid motion. The nature of the beast in him took over as his fangs sank deeply into the shark and he drank his fill. His secret was safe for now.

    Melanna heard her name being called from different directions. She was finally reunited with her friends who were scouring the beach for her. After seeing Melanna's torn clothes, they knew they were in for a story. The girls continued down the beach in the direction they were headed in the first place before the separation. After a good night's sleep, the young women were ferried off the island and started the trip back home. Melanna felt a longing to stay, but she knew that she needed to return with the others. It was as if something had awakened inside of her. She was a different person somehow. And she never stopped thinking about Tez.

6. SIBLING RIVALRY

The young women returned to their own villages and towns without incident and just in time to miss a sudden nasty tropical storm that came through the Yucatan that evening. The dark clouds gave way to blue sky and bright sunshine the next morning. Melanna was anxious to share her adventures with Qaileen. So she tied her gold embroidered robe about her, ate a quick breakfast and headed to Qaileen's quarters. After knocking briefly at the door, she heard the warm, familiar voice inside.

"Yes? Good morning, my grown up princess! And how are you this fine morning?"

"Quite well, thank you. I had a great time on the trip!"

"Tell me all about it, please! I'm so proud of you in taking this step into your life!"

"Well, the priestess was interesting in explaining our heritage and responsibilities as Mayan women. I feel richer for the experience. And the island itself is really beautiful beyond words! The island was so full of beautiful wildflowers. They even grow in the tops of the trees!"

At this time, Melanna's sister, Eleuia, stood silently outside the doorway listening to their conversation.

Qaileen's eyes had that far away look in them as scenes of her Right of Passage played in her mind those many years ago. She was fashioning the fabric that Melanna had purchased for Bonfire Night. Pieces of it were scattered on the floor.

Melanna continued, "And I saw the most unusual sight: a man in his twenties was swimming with a big shark just beyond the surf! And the local people think it's great for tourism! He loves the attention and the free drinks. I *literally* stumbled into his home. He lives in a cave at the bottom of a cenote on the island."

"Oh, boy, you weren't hurt, were you?"

"The worst of it was scratches to my hands and my ribs. I did black out for a short time. But other than that, I'm okay. The man said that he was acquainted with my sister, Eleuia, one night in a tavern here in Coba. He made it sound like she hounded his heels in there. But he seemed like a respectable type of person to me. I don't understand why Eleuia persisted in throwing herself at him if he clearly wasn't interested."

Qaileen rolled her eyes a bit and shook her head as she said, "It's the thrill of the chase, my dear. Sometimes people think that they want what they can't have."

"He acted like he knew me already, although I can't imagine where or when. Believe me, if I would have been introduced to him, I would never forget his face. He said he would come visit me here in Coba."

Eleuia could stand it no longer and made her entrance.

"Good morning!"

She gave her sister a sidewise glance as if she were looking at a toad on a pavement. Her hair was chestnut brown that cascaded in waves about her shoulders, and her eyes were the color of dark honey. But her facial features reflected the character within which was haughtiness and superiority. She was her own biggest fan.

"So, sister, you made it back in one piece. You didn't do anything that I wouldn't have, did you?"

Eleuia wanted to maintain her superiority over her sister in one area: experience and bragging rights when it came to the opposite sex. She had already taken several lovers at an early age. This was her way of dealing with a nonexistent relationship with her father, King Teteneeka. She also had a huge hole in her heart just as Melanna did. But Eleuia chose other ways to fill it that weren't the wisest or the smartest. It was because of her royal status that she felt she could get anyone she wanted. She didn't stop to think that maybe her young lovers could brag that they had bedded royalty. This could only increase their allure to the other young women of Coba.

Melanna faced her sister with dread, something that only increased over time.

"If you are suggesting if I partied with strange men into the wee hours of the morning, no, I didn't do that."

"What a waste of a trip! No wonder you're still a virgin!" Eleuia scoffed with an amused smile on her face.

"Excuse me, and who invited you in here? And my virginity is none of your business! Besides one alley cat in this castle is enough! Someone has to act like a responsible adult here and it might as well be me!"

"Ladies! Ladies!" Quaileen intervened.

"Anyway, I managed to almost get myself killed because I had to satisfy my curiosity. I guess you could say I had a near death experience by almost drowning in a deep cenote - one of the largest I've ever seen. The fall alone could have killed me! It was as if a spirit lured me in there and my personal angel saved me." A brief smile touched her lips as she reminisced.

Eleuia looked amused as she said, "Pray tell, what was this angel like?" She had a sneer on her face, confident that her sister could not match her charm or experience when it came to the opposite sex.

Melanna took a moment to bring up the memory of Tez that was so freshly etched in her mind, "Oh, about six feet one inch in height, wavy black hair, mesmerizing dark eyes, muscular build, and goes by the name of Tez."

Eleuia's eyes widened with a shock of realization. She remembered the face that went with that name. She also remembered how he had hurt her pride by refusing her. She tried every way she could to seduce him. Nothing seemed to faze him. He was immune to it all. Hurt now turned to anger to think that Tez would take an interest in the sister whom she detested.

Eleuia snorted with quiet humor, "My, my, yes! He's a big one! And how is it that you came to meet him?"

"I accidently fell into the cenote where he lives in a secret cave when he stays at Isla Cozumel."

A faint mocking smile was on Eleuia's lips as she said, "So he felt *obligated* to take care of you when you clumsily crashed into his private abode?"

"I was lucky that he was there to pull me out of the water. Who knows? I may have drowned when I blacked out if he hadn't rescued me." Her forehead wrinkled with her sister's interrogation. "Anyway, he asked if he could come visit me here in Coba. Naturally, I said 'yes'."

"You can't be seriously entertaining the thought that he is interested in you, are you? Look at you! You aren't the most popular girl and you certainly aren't the sexiest. I mean, let's face it. You *are* little-miss-home-body who enjoys the natural shabby look," Eleuia said with a demeaning smirk. "You really think that you stand a chance with this guy?" she said with a haughty look, batting her eyes for emphasis.

"Oh, there's no doubt in my mind that it could be a strong possibility. I think it's mutual really," Melanna said with newfound confidence with her chin jutting out and her head held high. She tried to turn her attention to the dress that Qaileen was making for her, ignoring her sister's comments. While she preoccupied herself with thoughts of Tez, she didn't notice that Eleuia fumed. "And besides, it's been a long time since I ran around the streets like a tom-boy, not caring what I looked like. I'm a young woman now. I've grown up and things have changed. I'm entitled to *someone* taking an interest in me! Besides, this is just one guy. What are you worried about? You have half of the guys in this city falling over you."

"Ya, well, we'll see how that plays out. If he proves to be too hot to handle, you can always come to me for advice." Eleuia tried to leave with her pride still intact.

"I don't think that'll be necessary, but thanks for the offer." Melanna said sarcastically.

"You know our father, the king, would most definitely disapprove of this vagabond coming here to the castle to court his daughter. You should forget that you ever met him," she said with a sneer.

"Why? So you can feel free to pursue him some more? You couldn't snag him when he had a few drinks in him. What makes you think you can do better with him sober?"

Eleuia gave her sister a swift viperous look and slithered out of the room. Quaileen took a deep breath as if a foul odor had left the room, and continued her cheerful conversation with Melanna. She waited until Eleuia's footsteps faded away and then she spoke.

"You know since you have come of age, I think that it is time that you learned some family history." Quaileen glanced quickly at Melanna while working on the dress to see her reaction.

"Like what kind of history? Are there any juicy secrets that I haven't been told?"

"Well, I won't bore you with your royal lineage, but I would like to tell you about your mother's side of the family. There have been some great warriors on that side of the family. There was nothing unusual or great about them. They came from a regular Mayan family. But when our people came under attack, they were suddenly quickened in body and spirit and made ready for battle as if they were always meant to be great warriors. There have been different times throughout Mayan history when raiders came to plunder and murder our people. They were drawn here by our abundance in gold and natural resources. But the warriors in your mother's bloodline were suddenly raised up to lead the attacks against our enemies."

"Wow. I wonder why father never told me about this."

"Melanna, you know as well as I do that he didn't take an active part in educating you. Besides, he has never been the warrior type himself."

"True! I wish that I could fall in love with one though."

"Maybe someday you will be lucky and meet a young handsome warrior who would give his life to defend you."

"Maybe I already have," she said with a mischievous smile on her face.

Melanna decided to spend time out in the garden behind the palace after her visit with Quaileen. She wanted to forget about how degrading her sister could treat her. When someone promising came along, Eleuia was there to burst her bubble. Why couldn't she have a normal sisterly relationship with her that other girls had with their sisters? Did Eleuia have such a low self-esteem that she needed to emotionally squash Melanna at every turn? She pondered these things as she came to the man-made lily pond that was an elevated stone structure at the center of the garden. The sunlight sparkled off the water in between the lily pads. Water lilies in a variety of pink and cream colors sprinkled the lily pond. Melanna bent over to smell a fragrant pink flower. Out of the corner of her eye she saw movement to her left. Across the gardens, lying on a bench was a young man who had been sleeping. He was clothed in an old brown robe with a hood. His face was smudged with dirt. Mud and dried leaves clung to his robe. He began to stir out of his sleep and caught Melanna staring at him with wide eyes and mouth open.

"I'm sorry. Did I scare you?" he asked. "I really didn't mean to. It was dark when I got here. This seemed like the most convenient place to catch a few winks."

"Do you have any idea where you are right now?"

"No, should I?" He slowly sat up and brushed some dirt from his face and robe. She could now see that he had a tattoo on his right cheek. The tattoo was in an unknown language that gave the meaning of his name.

الذي يشبه الرب

He threw his hood back to reveal a dark coppery mane of curls that were streaked by the sun and hung above his shoulders. His eyes were a steel blue, like the sky before a storm. She caught the sparkle of some small silver hoop earrings in his ears. She had never seen anyone quite like him and couldn't help but be somewhat mesmerized by his beauty.

"That's hard to believe. You just happen to be sleeping in the palace gardens owned by King Tetaneeka, ruler of Coba." She tapped her chin with her finger as she said, "I wonder what the penalty would be for someone who is loitering in the royal gardens?"

The stranger didn't act phased by this information. Instead, he came over to the lily pond, some several feet away from Melanna and asked, "May I?"

"May you what?"

"Freshen up a little?"

"Sure," she responded as she eyed him suspiciously.

Without hesitation, he flung his robe off, revealing broad shoulders, a muscular chest and arms. He sported a scroll-like tattoo in the middle of his chest that was black with curves and points, like gothic art. He scooted some lily pads out of his way as he cupped water in his hands to splash over his face. He proceeded to splash water over his chest and arms. And then he stood up, shook the dust from his robe, and dried himself off with it. Melanna caught a glimpse of a pair of giant tattooed angel wings on his back.

"So who exactly are you and what are you doing here?"

"Forgive me! My name is Micah," he said as he extended his hand for a handshake. His voice was deep, spoken with authority.

Melanna shook his hand with a bit of caution. Micah's expression became sober as visions of Melanna's future flashed through his mind like a fast moving picture show. Through her touch he saw the things to come. How could he explain to her his mission without her thinking she was entertaining a crazy man?

He kept his composure friendly as he said, "I have an avid interest in traveling. I make my way by helping people out in exchange for food and shelter."

Micah rummaged around in his pocket and pulled out some sweet red lychee fruits that had been squashed while sleeping on them. He pulled some fuzzy debris off of them and popped them in his mouth.

Melanna wrinkled her nose while observing his eating habits. She turned and walked several paces along the edge of the water garden to put some distance between her and the stranger.

"It may not seem like the best life to you, but at least I'm free. No one tells me what to do and how to do it. And I get to experience other cultures around the world. And may I ask who you are?"

"I'm princess Melanna. This is my home."

"Wow. What are the chances of me meeting up with you in this grand city?" he said with pretend surprise.

"Really!" Melanna wondered if it was really chance that brought him here as she looked away and blinked before meeting his gaze again.

Micah went on, as he tousled his wet hair, "I'm not only a traveler. I am also a public speaker of sorts. I tend to show up before life altering doom and destruction."

"You're kidding me, right?"

He stopped tousling his hair to look her in the eyes as he said charmingly, "Now would I do that to such a beautiful princess who was so kind enough to let me have the use of her water garden?" His eyes roamed over her as his head rested on his folded arms on the edge of the stones.

"No, I guess not." She switched her weight on her feet nervously as she said, "I'm not aware of any 'doom and destruction' going on around here. What makes you think that there is any such thing taking place now or in the future?"

"It is my gift," he said with a shrug, "it is what I do. That's my purpose in life, at least one of them."

Melanna wanted to change the subject and not completely ruin her day by thinking of doom and destruction.

"So am I to understand that you are looking for work and place to-"

Micah was standing in front of her, having not made a sound as he drew near. He stood two feet from her. His sudden closeness caught her by surprise.

"Yes, do you know where I could make some money while I stay here a short time in Coba?"

"Well, since you seem to like the garden so much, would you like to help out with the gardening?" she asked with a shrug of her shoulder. He nodded. "And you can sleep and dine with the other servants in the palace. Does that suit you?"

"Yes, my lady, that sounds like a gracious offer."

She stared into his eyes for a brief moment and said, "Good. I will let Zolin know that you are hired on. He is the old man servant that answers directly to the king and oversees the servants. So come and report to him tomorrow morning."

Micah gave a slight bow of acknowledgement.

"Princess, I-"

"Please call me Melanna. Everyone does."

"Melanna, I can sense that you don't believe me when I say that I come with a message."

She shrugged and said, "I just met you. I don't have a clue about you or your message. Don't mistake my caution for unbelief."

"Let me just say that there is coming a very powerful enemy of your people. You will play a big role in defeating the enemy, but it will come with certain losses. That is all I will say for now."

Melanna looked away at the horizon for a brief second. When she glanced back, he was gone. A large black feather lay on the ground where Micah once stood. She turned to her right and saw Micah quite a ways away from her. He glanced over his shoulder at her and waved goodbye. She just shook her head thinking what a strange one he is. She bent down, picked the feather up, and proceeded to walk through the garden at a lingering pace as all of her senses took in the beauty, sunshine and fragrances.

But the image of Micah and the mystery of him refused to be pushed out of her mind. She especially wondered if she could put much stock in his message. If what he said was true.

7. THE STRANGER CAME KNOCKING

A week went slowly by. King Teteneeka made a trip to Tulum on the coast of the Caribbean Sea for two reasons. The first one was to pay his merchants a visit that did Coba's importing and exporting. And the second reason was to join other people of royalty from other provinces for a short vacation. They had the best entertainment that royalty could buy, such as beautiful dancing girls. And of course, the wine flowed freely. The rugged beauty of the cliffs along the white beaches and the pristine temples would be lost on such people who visited.

The next morning after Teteneeka's departure to Tulum, Melanna was curious at how Micah was working out as one of the gardening staff. She approached one of the old gardeners who had spent years serving king Tenaneeka.

"Good morning! How is Micah working out for you?"

"I have never in my days seen such gifted hands in the garden as that young man. He has a way with our most difficult plantings. Even the dying ones seem to come alive and thrive at his very touch! See here."

The old gardener waved his hand at a flowering archway and a shrub that they had wanted to dig up and throw away. Not to mention the diseased fruit trees that they had given up on. All were flowering and bearing fruit.

"He is a gift from heaven!" exclaimed the old gardener as he stood there with his hands clasped over his chest and shaking his head.

"You're probably more right about that than you'll ever know."

She strolled over to the lily pond and once again admired the beautiful blooms. Then she noticed the reflection of Micah looking at her and smiling. She looked up and around her. He was nowhere to be found. Melanna picked up a small stone and hurled it at the reflection. After the ripples had settled, the image was gone. She smiled to herself.

You crazy girl. Maybe you've had too much sun.

She went to her room and decided to spend some time relaxing in her laid-back comfortable clothing. After some time passed, there was a knock at the door of the palace. An old man servant, Zolin, opened the door to find Tez standing there looking well groomed with a single pink orchid in his hand. He was wearing tan pants, a woven white shirt and sandals. He also wore silver cuff bracelets on each wrist with a stamped design of a dancing eagle. His bronze chest peaked out from the open shirt with the ever-present silver talisman dangling on its chain.

"Is the Lady Melanna in this morning?"

"Come in, Sir, and I will summon her for you."

Tez was ushered into the great hall as he waited for Melanna. When Zolin found Melanna in her room, she was in her unflattering clothes and her hair was a mess. She was lying on her tummy reading a book. When she was told that Tez was waiting for her, she sat up in a panic and cried out to Qaileen to help her find something suitable to put on in a hurry. They settled on a cobalt blue, gauzy dress with a wide leather belt. A white shell necklace and matching bracelet completed the look. Qaileen chased after Melanna with a comb in hand. Melanna slid her feet into her sandals and calmly made her way to the great hall. There standing several feet from the entrance was Tez. Melanna's heart jumped into her throat.

Zolin gestured with his left hand toward the visitor as he announced, "Tezcatli Uetzcayotl".

"But you know me best as Tez".

There was something commanding about his very presence. Something in his eyes that made him above everything, on another level.

"Thank you, Zolin. You may go now," Melanna said, anxious to be alone once again with the dark stranger.

Tez looked Melanna over with appraising eyes until they met her own.

"Just the sight of you was worth the trip here, if I may be so bold to say. And under much better circumstances too." He gave Melanna the pink orchid, which she gladly accepted. She inhaled its perfume. "I hope that you don't mind that I dropped in unexpectedly, pardon the pun." He gave her a teasing smile.

"Well, it is an unexpected surprise, but a welcome one."

"I thought that you could introduce me to some of your favorite places here in Coba. And then we could get to know each other by a warm fire. Or maybe we could just wing it and let fate lead us where it may," he said with a shrug to his right shoulder." All the while his eyes looked into hers as if he were looking into her soul, seeing her like no one else had ever seen her. He appreciated her beautiful as well.

Melanna could feel the heat of his gaze and blushed.

"All of that sounds good to me. So where do we start?"

"I think that there are some festivities going on in the marketplace today. A group of people from the Caribbean are providing entertainment and selling their wares there. It should be fun. How about it?" he asked as he leaned casually against the wall beside the door.

"Of course! I love to see that kind of stuff. That sounds great. I think we should head over there."

Melanna tugged on the massive entrance door. Tez placed his hand on the door above her head to pull it open for her. His face was near her hair as he breathed in the scent of her. The nearness of her and the scent of her filled his cold being like the effect of the sun shining through a window, which brings warmth and cheer. But why did she have to smell so tempting? It's a good thing that he fed before coming to see her. He now had better control of his urges. Tez pulled the door open and secured it closed behind them.

They made their way into the perfect day. The balmy breezes caught their hair and clothing, making them ripple in the wind.

Getting around Coba was made easier by the network of raised walkways built of stone called sacbeob. Coba had more of them than any Mayan city. Before they knew it, they were there at the marketplace amongst the throng of people and watching Caribbean dancing. The dancing took place under a huge open-air building with a thatched roof and a platform. The male dancers whirled rapidly and twirled blazing torches to the swift beat of drums. The island men were bare-chested, and adorned themselves with wooden necklaces and a band of green leaves in their hair. They worked themselves into a sweat with their dancing. Their dance was both a story of survival and celebration. They even threw in a few flips and cartwheel kicks. The crowd was in awe. Melanna was no exception.

Wow, with Tez sharing this moment with me, I'm enjoying this even more than I would have otherwise.

She gave him an appreciative look. He gave her a half smile and nodded in return.

They stayed through a couple more dances, one in which young beautiful girls did a traditional island dance. They were nude from the hips up, but their long, dark hair covered their breasts. The girls wore grass skirts, accentuated by tuffs around the hips. Again, their dance was like a story that was told by their hands and the movement of their bodies. Melanna couldn't help comparing their vibrant beauty to her own, feeling rather plain in comparison. But she felt a strong hand gently take her own with a small squeeze of reassurance. She looked up at Tez who gave her a quick wink. She suddenly felt warm all over although Tez's hand was cooler than her own hand. And suddenly the dance was over. The crowd applauded and broke up. Melanna was still lost in the moment.

Tez cleared his throat and said, "You must be thirsty after that long walk here from the palace. How 'bout I find some cool drinks?"

"Yes, please. Thanks." Melanna rolled her eyes as he turned to leave.

Pull yourself together!

Why did she feel like a candle being consumed by a flame when he was around? What made him so intriguing? It was definitely his eyes. No, it was the way he seemed to look into her very soul. Or was it because he was in tune with her feelings and knew just what to say? She shook her head to clear it and tried to think of something else unsuccessfully.

Tez went to a nearby vendor and returned with two drinks that resembled a fruit punch. Melanna chugged hers down in no time while Tez did not touch his at all, his eyes never leaving Melanna. She sat there looking at him with narrowed eyes and one eyebrow cocked up.

"You haven't touched your drink!"

"No, I'm not really thirsty. But I see that you're ready for another one. Have mine." He slid it over to her. She smiled and started to sip this one slower.

He decided to start a conversation with her, pretending to want to know about her family when in fact he already knew a great deal about them. After the death of the queen, Tez was always vigilant, not far away from baby Melanna through the years as she grew up. For instance, if a jaguar came too close to where she played, he always intervened, driving the hungry creature away. He kept within earshot of her cries and a watchful eye of her mishaps, all the while never revealing himself to her or any of the household. But he did fulfill his promise to the queen.

His thoughts came back to the present as Melanna went on, "…And my father, well, what can I say? He's the king. He doesn't have much time for me. I am much closer to Qaileen, my servant from birth. She knows me and loves me best. And I can truly say that I love her. She is like a mother to me."

"I'm sorry to hear about your mother, Melanna. I've heard stories about what an incredible woman she was. I'm sure that you will be, in fact, may be just like her both in beauty and in character."

The heat rose to Melanna's cheeks. "Thank you. I am honored that I'm deserving of such praise. Forgive me, I'm not use to such compliments" she looked down at her hands, clearly not used to being the center of attention.

Tez seized the awkward moment with a suggestion, "How 'bout you show me one of your favorite local places that you love to visit?" Of course, he already knew what place she would take him, but he continued to play the unwitting date. He stood up and offered his hand to help her up on her feet. They continued down the main road of the marketplace, and after a few turns, ended up in a secluded garden with a large reflecting pool in the center. It was a bird sanctuary of sorts, for there seemed to be every species of native bird to inhabit the small piece of real estate. The grounds were well taken care of too. It proved to be the favorite spot for many other people as well. There was a bench under a shade tree that they rested on. Two blue and green colored parrots shared a tree branch to the right above them.

"Can you tell me something, anything about your own family?"

Tez's countenance changed suddenly as if he were visiting a time and a place that he didn't want to visit. He took a few seconds to decide what he felt he could share with her at this time.

"I came from an average middle class family in the Northern part of the Yucatan. I helped my father farm or put fish on the table. My mother weaved traditional garments and fabrics for some additional income." He paused to look into her eyes and went on. "When I turned twenty-three, I fell in love with the most beautiful girl of my village. I was thrilled when she wanted to marry me. We were on our honeymoon when we were unfortunate to run into trouble. We were attacked by a savage group of people from a bloodthirsty cult." His eyes flicked to hers briefly and then he continued. "They killed my new bride and left me for dead."

Melanna gasped and covered her mouth with her right hand.

"I lost everyone that ever mattered to me: my mother, my father and the woman I loved. They didn't stop there. They decimated my whole village before leaving the area. There were only a few people left alive."

Tez's voice cracked with emotion as he told his story. Even though this had occurred two hundred years ago, it was still very hard for him to relive these events of his mortal life.

A deep sadness came over Melanna. The story stirred her blood.

Oh my gosh, what a first date this is turning out to be! Me and my big mouth. Her eyes misted over as she looked intently at the ground. "I'm so very sorry to hear about your loss."

Tez took his finger and lifted her chin in order for her to look at him as he solemnly said, "Thank you. I wasn't sure how you would react to my past, especially about the part that I was married."

Melanna returned his gaze with sad eyes.

"It is no surprise that a guy who is as handsome as you are, had found a mate early in life. True love is a rare and beautiful thing. But what kind of people could do such an awful thing to you and your people?"

"Very powerful, very wicked people, without mercy. Perhaps without a soul. They are more like demons walking the earth, bent on destroying people for their own wicked pleasure. Or perhaps they just have an appetite for such things. Pray you never see such creatures in your life time." He took a deep breath before he went on. "I should have died that day, but I didn't. Oh, how I wanted to! I had no reason or desire to go on living afterwards. I felt like a tortured spirit walking the earth among the dead. Days passed and a small group of men came to my village. They helped me bury the dead. And they shared their faith in the Great Spirit with me. I was a man without his people, without parents. But I have embraced a new philosophy that gives me hope: I am now a son of the Great Spirit by adoption through faith. And I now have an extended family, the ones who helped me. We use this symbol of the eagle for our new life," as he pointed to the stamped design on one of his chunky, silver cuff bracelets of the dancing eagle. Melanna couldn't see the connection between the eagle and his faith in the Great Spirit.

"What does this symbol mean?"

"The ancient writings say that with the Great Spirit old things will pass away; all things become new; and He will 'renew our strength like the eagle's'". The sorrow that hung over them with the retelling of the story was lifted with his message of hope. A peaceful moment was shared between them. They gazed into each other's eyes. She was wishing that she could erase his painful history. He was wishing that he could tell her the complete story of what transformed him into an immortal, a child of night. Someday, but it wouldn't be today.

The chatter of young people strolling through the garden distracted them. Melanna saw a few friends from school that she gave a quick greeting to. They in turn looked curiously at her date and whispered amongst their friends. Their whisperings couldn't be heard by Melanna, but Tez could hear them as if they stood close by. He smiled at their compliments. Their gazes turned to him as he smiled at them. This made them feel uneasy. The group made a quick departure.

Tez and Melanna continued to enjoy the garden until after the sun went down. She assured Tez that dinner would be waiting for her when she returned to the palace. There would be no need to grab a bite on the way home.

Tez and Melanna walked slowly down the darkened streets of Coba toward the castle. They had just passed a pub where a few patrons were standing just outside the door. The place reeked of stale beer and vomit. A couple was kissing, the woman being flattened against the wall of the establishment. Tez and Melanna made their way passed them and through the debris on the street. As they approached a dark alley, a menacing looking man approached them with a knife in his hand. He demanded all of their money. Melanna clutched Tez's arm as she stood behind him trembling.

Tez remained calm and spoke to Melanna to try to calm her, "This is the reason why people should not venture out at night especially near these establishments. You never know what loathsome creatures are creeping around here." His eyes slowly left Melanna to meet the robber's stare at the end of his statement for emphasis.

The stranger didn't find it humorous at all as he replied, "Listen, buddy, I haven't got all night! Hand it over! Now!"

Tez looked almost amused as he said, "Sorry, friend, I'm not giving up my money to a pathetic excuse of a human being like you! Do you think that waving that knife in someone's face makes you a bigger man? You remind me of a little boy who is squealing for some attention-"

"Shut, up! I'm not going to ask you again!"

"As I was saying, sir, please try not to do anything that you may regret. Just let us go about our business."

Melanna's eyes were wide with fear. She forced a swallow down her dry throat. Her rapid heartbeat could be heard by Tez only. It sounded like that of a bird in a nest that was cornered by a snake.

"Hey, buddy, who's holding the knife here? Maybe I'll just have to cut your girl since you're not cooperating-."

Tez's eyes became fiendishly dark as he interjected, "I'm going to have to ask you again, don't do anything stupid. I'd hate for you to lose the use of your arm," he prodded with a crooked smile. But the fierce challenging look in his eyes said that he was not joking.

The stranger lunged at Tez with the knife. With lightening speed Tez gently pushed Melanna away as he whirled behind the stranger. The knife clamored to the ground. Suddenly Tez had the robbers arm straight out and twisted at an angle as the man was bent over on his knees. Then a terrible bone-crunching sound came as the man howled in pain. Patrons outside of the pub were frightened and scattered in different directions.

Tez leaned forward and whispered into the robber's ear, "This should teach you not to mistreat a lady! And if I ever see you in these parts again, well, we'll just have to see what else I can break!" Tez stood the robber up, grabbed the man's head with one hand, and bashed it against the stone wall, sending the man into unconsciousness. The robber crumbled to the ground.

Melanna stood there with her mouth open in shock at what she had just witnessed. She could not will her feet to move.

Tez turned his attention to her and said, "Are you okay? Are you hurt?"

He got no response from her. She was still processing what just happened. Tez closed the gap and put his arms around her, assuring her that she was safe. She trembled inside of his embrace. He told her to take deep breaths. When he pulled away, Melanna gasped at the sight of blood. The knife had slashed the right bicep of Tez's arm.

"Don't worry about it. It's just a scratch." He fumbled with his torn shirt and snorted, "This was one of my favorite shirts! You know, if that guy weren't unconscious already, I'd break-"

"I think that I'll have Qaileen look at that when we get back to the palace," Melanna said while taking him by the hand and leading him away.

They walked hurriedly through the streets. Once inside the palace, she had Qaileen see to his injury. Melanna paced the floor a total of four times when Qaileen came out to speak to her.

"Child, can you please stop playing pranks on me and wasting my time?"

"What do you mean by that?"

"I mean that I don't see an injury on Tezcotli just now."

"What? What do you mean 'no injury'? I'm certain that I saw an injury on his arm with my own eyes. I saw plenty of blood on him outside the pub there!"

"Yes, but it was dark, right? Maybe it was from your attacker."

"No, if anything, that guy got a broken arm and a huge lump on his head." Melanna placed her hand over her forehead and tried to remember. "Well, it *was* dark. Maybe it was the other man's blood. I can't be sure."

A shirtless Tez came out of the room and into the hall. The subtle light of the evening lamps played over the muscles of his lean, muscular body. Both women stood there mesmerized by the unearthly beauty of the man before them. He took their breath away.

"Are you ladies done making a fuss over me? May I go home now? Or is there anything else on me that you'd like to examine?"

Both women closed their mouths and composed themselves. He looked at Melanna out of the corner of his eyes as the left side of his mouth curved into a smile. Melanna looked away out of embarrassment and bit her lower lip. Quaileen pretended to fuss with her hair.

Qaileen answered, "I guess you can go. I appreciate you looking after Melanna tonight, sir. I'm in your debt."

Tez pulled his shirt over his head. Melanna walked to his side, took his arm in hers and walked him to the door. After Qaileen was out of sight, she thought it best to have a word with Tez before he left. They stepped outside the door and closed it for privacy. There were things that Melanna wanted to discuss with Tez, but now was not the time or place.

"I don't know what to say. 'Thank you' just doesn't seem to cover it. When can I see you again?"

"You really want to see me again after what happened today? I didn't frighten you off?"

"You'll have to work a lot harder than that to frighten *me* off!"

Tez took Melanna's hand and kissed the inside of her palm. His hand held her face as he gazed into her eyes in the moon light.

"I'll see you soon. Good night, princess."

He kissed her cheek before turning to leave. His kisses made her shiver with anticipation.

8. BONFIRE NIGHT

The few remaining days of school passed quickly until Bonfire Night had finally arrived. This signaled the end of the school year. All of the young people were so excited about the festivities of the evening. There was a great feast followed by a night of dancing and celebration.

It was interesting to see who showed up as a couple at Bonfire Night, not that it meant they were promised to each other. It was a status thing. This night was not meant to discuss what you plan to do with the rest of your life. This night was to be lived right now, in the moment, with your favorite people by your side.

When Manny came to the palace to accompany Melanna to Bonfire Night, she took his breath away. Never had she been as beautiful in all the years that he'd known her. He was use to seeing her running with the other kids with a dirty face and hair looking wild as they played games. But she was all grown up now, looking every inch a woman in that dress. Manny had also matured through the years to become a strong and handsome young man, well-muscled, medium build, tall, and dark-haired. But not as tall and muscular as Tez, Melanna noted to herself.

One of his dark brown eyes was always hidden behind a thick strand of jet-black hair over the left side of his face. He closed his mouth and tried to compose himself as he greeted her. She flashed him a smile and knew that her charms were working on him. Nelli and Yoltzin stood arm in arm, waiting for them at the front door of the palace as were Zonya and Teela.

When they arrived at the field of the bonfire festivities, the young men worked together to assemble the logs to be burned. The sunset was fading fast. The fire was lit and fueled underneath by smaller logs and debris. The crowd applauded their approval.

Nelli in her red tiered skirt and white festive blouse took center stage to give her speech as the top student in her class. She was well spoken and everyone liked her.

"Life is what you make of it so live your dreams. But more important than your dreams, be a person of compassion. For it is the love and compassion in your life that will carry you through any circumstance. Cherish the people in your life: your friends, your family and even strangers. Take the opportunities that life gives you and make the most out of it because we'll never pass this way again."

The audience applauded and cheered. The musicians started to play as everyone feasted on the great food and drink provided for this event. Young people slipped away from the tables to dance with their dates around the bonfire as darkness fell. When almost everyone had finished eating, it was time for the group dance. It was a tradition to dance the wheel dance on Bonfire Night. The musicians started playing the spirited music on conch shell trumpets, drums, maracas, and ceramic flutes. The young men formed several circles while the girls formed an inner circle inside each of these groups. When the music began, the circles of girls weaved in and out of the circle of the boys, but not before being dipped and twirled about by the boy to her right before going on to the next boy to her right. This was all done in unison. It was so much fun. A girl could definitely meet a new guy this way. Such was the case of Zonya when the dance ended and she was left looking into the face of Noctli. He was taller than any boy in school and really cute too. His name meant "prickly pear fruit". The kids at school thought he lived up to his name. His personality was such as you either liked him or you couldn't stand the guy because he had such a prickly personality. Zonya hadn't had the pleasure of knowing Noctli until this night. She smiled at him and thanked him before releasing their dance hold. Noctli recognized a pretty girl when he saw one, so he asked her if he could accompany her for the rest of the evening. Zonya obliged him but secretly wished that he wouldn't say or do anything that would spoil the evening. After all, his reputation preceded him. They both walked over to a quieter place to get to know each other while they watched the festivities from a distance.

Noctli started out by saying, "I've noticed you at school. You're always with your friends so it's been hard for me to approach you. I'm glad that I had this opportunity tonight."

"Ya, I've seen you at school too, especially in sports. Your parents must be very proud of you," said Zonya with shy eyes only meeting his briefly. She tucked her dark wavy hair behind her ear and smoothed her green and white-tiered skirt on her lap.

"Well, I don't have a father. He left me, my mom, my little sister years ago. And this past year my mother has been very sick. I've been working a job to support all of us during non-school hours. You can imagine how hard is to be equally good at either one. That may be the reason why I'm hard to get along with sometimes. I've been burning my candle at both ends," said Noctli with the right side of his mouth ending in a smirk after having admitted the reason why he acts the way he does.

Zonya was shocked at this revelation and had a new appreciation for this guy sitting next to her. She never really noticed his strong, handsome profile until tonight, sitting this close to him. The rest of him wasn't bad either. She suddenly felt safe and trusting of him. She opened up to him, telling him about her ordinary life and her unordinary friends. Noctli thought that he could use some good friends in his life. He had really been too busy to make any friends. If they were as great as Zonya, his social life would change considerably.

Meanwhile, Melanna and Manny were dancing the night away in each other's arms while they smiled and waved to friends they passed. While Melanna danced in Manny's embrace, she could have sworn that she saw Micah sitting by himself, watching the festivities as the glow of the bonfire lit his face and his deep coppery colored hair. Melanna stopped dancing as she remained in Manny's arms. She stared into the eyes of Micah.

She could hear a voice inside of her head saying, "Remember my message to you. It all begins now."

Melanna shook her head. Micah was gone. Manny was bewildered.

"What's wrong? Are you alright?"

"I'm okay. I thought I saw something."

"Maybe we should sit down awhile and catch our breath."

No one noticed the dark beautiful figure that stood on the other side of the bonfire, watching all of the merriment from afar. She had the look of a seductive predator, with almond shaped eyes and red lips set into a perfect oval shaped face. Zafrina and her followers had come into the city just days before without any attention drawn to them. They observed how many people there were, their way of life and their religious beliefs. There were people to prey upon and to quench their thirst; and people that would fear and worship them. The Dark One would make them fear her. The mood of the stranger brewed and was as if the weather reflected those feelings. Dark stormy clouds gathered right above the celebration. Lightening flickered and thunder rumbled overhead. Some people responded by finding some shelter. Others ignored it and kept dancing in the rain. The beautiful immortal walked slowly up to the bonfire and then started to ascend to the top of it, light as air. Her robes fanned out behind her like a great dark bird. The flames licked her body as if she had just come from hell itself and was immune to the heat while her eyes glowed with hot rage. The Dark One compelled the crowd to receive her message.

"Be warned. The prosperity of your kingdom will soon come to an end. Death and destruction will plague your kingdom unless you follow the way of human sacrifice. A New Age is upon you. Follow me in obedience or pay the ultimate price. Make your choice."

The wind suddenly became violent, tearing at everyone's hair and clothing. A funnel cloud enveloped the bonfire and trailed after the cloaked figure as she ascended from the top of the flames into the dark clouds above. Flashes of lightening and a deafening clap of thunder followed. Those cold, unfeeling eyes seemed to be etched in the clouds to continue to watch the mortals with scorn. It was as if Zafrina and the storm were one and the same. Evil laughter echoed across the sky. As the strong gale winds continued to blow, hail started to pelt the crowd. Small fires licked the ground here and there, mixed with the deluge of hail. Everyone ran for cover.

Melanna and Manny crouched under a little thatched roof nearby. They stood there, speechless and trembling. Did they really see what they just saw: a goddess riding the flames and then ascending into the clouds? What kind of creature was she that she could control the elements? Someone to be feared, no doubt.

Needless to say, the uninvited guest put a halt to the festivities of the night. As the frightened humans ran in different directions, the tables were overturned, spilling the food and drink that were left out in the deluge. The bonfire was no match for the rain. The flames were soon extinguished by the storm sending up white smoke instead.

Word spread quickly throughout the city about the angry goddess who hovered above the flames and commanded the fury of the storm. An emergency meeting was held in the conference hall of the palace where the city officials and religious leaders discussed the message of the goddess. The majority agreed that more proof was needed before drastic measures were taken. Some feared the outcome of this meeting. And so it was that the next day was the beginning of a long, hot drought. The drought threatened the people's very existence. This was followed by a mysterious plague that started to kill the livestock. It was the kind of plague that left no blood in the animals. What kind of plague could do that? The people turned to Zafrina who insisted that human sacrifice was the only way to appease the gods and to restore the bounty they once knew. Most of the time, if they had enemies in their prisons in Coba, then prisoners would be sacrificed. If there were no prisoners, some unfortunate person among the kingdom was selected for sacrifice, and it was usually one who opposed Zafrina. No one was safe and no one was excluded. A pseudo miracle came when the crops started to grow again and the plague on the cattle ceased. A great pyramid was erected at the request of Zafrina. It served as personal chambers for her and her closest attendants known as the Ancients. It also served for human sacrifice. Gold, precious gems and decadent detail went into building the pyramid.

The idea of human sacrifice began to become popular with the people, especially among the youth. Some saw it as a stimulating carnal desire. To witness the taking of human life and to satisfy one's own lust for blood was a "rush". Others thought that euthanasia of the old was a concept whose time had come. Sacrificial jewelry was starting to be worn by the youth, such as a tiny dagger with a red stained blade adorning one's neck. Children were now being taught at school how it would be the highest honor to be counted as one that was selected for sacrifice on behalf of the people. Teachers lead students to sing songs of praise to the Goddess of the Moon for being a savior to their people.

Zafrina struck at the heart of their religion by eliminating the most trusted religious leaders. Mortals were like sheep that could be lead anywhere. Why not lead them to slaughter? All she had to do was show them a few cattle drained of blood and some freakish weather events and they all became obedient servants. Religious leaders started disappearing throughout the city. Only a few people inquired about this, but most were drawn into the Sacrificial New Age religion established by Zafrina. After all, it was either that or the Mayan people would perish, so they thought. Actually, they would perish either way. One way was slow and selective. The other way, to resist, affected the people's very existence on a larger scale.

Next Zafrina moved on to eliminate respected political leaders of the city, that is, except for King Tetaneeka who was her willing confidant. Anything to please the Goddess of the Moon, for He thought he was protecting the people and their way of life. But he didn't see the larger picture. His people were perishing. His people were enslaved to a demon. He was not the one in control any more. Tetaneeka became her willing puppet. Some people recognized this, but were too afraid to speak out lest they become the next victim to be sacrificed. So the resistance stayed silent, but they grew in number and in resilience.

9. ESCAPING REALITY

School commencement followed a few days after Bonfire Night. It was very low key due to the fact that morale was way down after Zafrina and her Ancients took over the city of Coba. The ceremony was simple and over quickly. Hugs were exchanged between friends with tearful faces. And promises were given to remain in touch. Best friends would always remain very good friends throughout life.

After commencement, anxiety filled Melanna's heart. Was life really so complicated or do we each hold the power of our future by the choices we make? Hours turned to days. Days turned into weeks. Then one morning Melanna woke to a perfect day after an overnight tropical storm had passed through. She poked her head out the window of the palace and watched the servants as they picked up debris and palm trees fronds that the wind had strewn everywhere.

Tez was vigilant at the edge of the jungle. He was perched on the branch of a massive monkey pod tree. He spied Melanna at once and smiled to himself. Melanna ducked back inside and decided that she would leave the cares of the world behind her today. She would get dressed and enjoy the outdoors. The more wilderness, the better. She chose a sleeveless top and mid-length purple woven skirt and sandals. The color complimented her bronze skin tone. She went to the kitchen and tossed some fruit, some tortillas and meat into a basket to eat on the way. Before she could reach the front door of the castle, a heavy knocking came. Zolin opened the door and found Tez asking if the Lady Melanna was in. Melanna set her basket on the floor of the great hall as she welcomed Tez and held her hands out to him in greeting. He clasped her hands with his cool ones, which sent little shivers down her spine. But his smile warmed her. The blood flowed to her face, making her even more beautiful. Tez wore a deep v-neck tunic with his dark blue woven pants. The ever present silver talisman dangled on his chest. Was it possible for this man to be even more handsome than before? Or was it because her feelings for him grew inside her heart?

"Great timing! I was just about to go hiking through the jungle this morning. I just need to get out of here for awhile. Would you like to come along?" He stood looking at her, his dark eyes brown eyes checking her out.

"Sorry, I'm a bit under dressed." she continued, "I wasn't expecting anybody."

"You're perfect." He said and meant it with all his heart.

Eleuia just happened to come around the corner into the great hall.

"Well, if it isn't Tezcotli. What a nice surprise," she said in a sarcastic tone. She gave him a smug smile and then continued. "And how is it that we are so honored with your presence?"

"I'm here to take your gorgeous sister out for a picnic this morning. This wild orchid pales in comparison to Melanna's beauty. But still, I didn't want to come empty handed."

Melanna took the flower from his hand and inhaled its fragrance.

"I just feel privileged to accompany her today. I know a treasure when I see one." He didn't give Eleuia the satisfaction of looking at her as he spoke. His eyes never left Melanna's face.

Eleuia's face was full of disgust and mockery, "I think I'm gonna puke! Please. You can't be serious-"

"Oh, but I am." It was as if his eyes could see right through her. "You know, that shade of green just doesn't become you, Eleuia," he said as cool as he could, mocking her. His gaze returned to Melanna as he brought her hand to his lips with a kiss. More heat rose to Melanna's face causing her to blush. She felt so elated that it felt like her feet were off the ground. Her heart beat unevenly. Tez took Melanna's left hand and guided her to the door. Melanna, with her basket in hand, looked back at her sister who was standing there with her mouth open in unbelief.

Melanna said, "What's the matter, sister? Sour grapes again?" She giggled on her way out.

Eleuia seethed silently, watching them disappear.

And then under her breath she said, "Ya, you'll get what's coming to you real soon! I promise."

Although Tez and Melanna were far enough away for the average person not to her Eleuia's last comment, Tez could hear it just fine. He made a mental note of it. This was something more serious than sibling rivalry. Eleuia could potentially be a threat to Melanna in some way in the future. But it was time to enjoy the moment with this beautiful young woman...who was waving at another guy who had a silly grin on his face. Manny was walking toward Melanna and gave her a hug and a kiss on the cheek. As they stood there embracing, Manny gave a quick glance at Tez from over Melanna's shoulder, his smile quickly fading. Tez felt a rush of jealousy just then. He could easily throttle this young pup, toss his body in the jungle, and no one would be the wiser. Melanna placed her hands on Manny's chest and distanced herself from him. She suddenly felt awkward to be the center of attention of the two young men standing before her. So she tried to make the best of the situation by inviting Manny to come along.

"Would you like to join us for a picnic in the jungle this morning?"

Manny raked the dark, straight hair out of his face with his fingers, and said, "It depends. What's in the basket?"

"Beggars can't be choosers."

"In that case, you can surprise me. You know I'll eat anything," he said as he looked at her out of the corner of his eyes and then turned his gaze to Tez.

"I'm sorry. Manny this is Tez. Tez this is Manny. Manny has been my friend since childhood. He accompanied me to the Bonfire Night a couple of weeks ago -"

"Speaking of which, did you happen to hear what went down that night when that freakish lady did that parlor trick?" He addressed his question to Tez.

"Hmm. I understand that it was no parlor trick. She's the real deal. What do you make of it?" Tez knew everything about the immortals, but he wanted to know what was being talked about.

"It's either do or die. That's what it appears to be. Everyone is giving her what she wants, including the king. There's nothing that we can do."

"There's always something a person can do. You just have to know the right people. We shouldn't lose hope."

Manny mistook Tez's confidence as being cocky. But Tez knew that there was a cure for the evil that plagued the city. But the cure would demand a great price. Freedom was never free.

The three of them made their way into the jungle along a worn path. The animals and birds made the jungle alive with their songs wafting in the breeze. A group of black howler monkeys acted agitated that people would invade their territory. Several males made their guttural loud sound as the monkeys stood their ground in the trees. The sound resembled loud angry bears, not the cute monkey sounds one would think.

The tall trees allowed some filtered sunlight through. The heat and humidity caused Manny and Melanna to be covered in perspiration, although Tez didn't seem to be affected by the warm climate at all. The jungle was a sea of green. Trees, flowers and tropical foliage competed for space in the jungle, along with wild vines that grew everywhere. When they came into a small clearing, Melanna unpacked her breakfast basket. She wondered out loud if it was a good idea to make a fire. At once the two young men went looking for firewood. Manny returned with an armload of small branches. The smile fell from his face when he saw that Tez carried a whole tree into the clearing.

"What on earth?" Melanna said with a smile on her face.

"What? Too much?" Tez asked with his hands raised, palms up.

"Just a little, don't you think?"

"Nah!"

Tez swiftly broke the tree into pieces while his audience marveled at the speed and strength that he exhibited. Then he stopped briefly to pretend that he was winded. But to overdo it anymore would bring suspicion on him, if it hadn't already.

Melanna, with her eyes fixed on Tez shook her head with a smile. She unpacked the food from the basket and realized that there wasn't enough for all three of them to eat.

"Do you guys think that we need more meat to go with this meal? I don't think I brought enough."

Manny immediately whittled a branch into a spear and speared a couple of fish in a nearby stream. Tez disappeared into the deep jungle only to reappear with a whole deer draped over his shoulders. Melanna stood with her hands on her hips, shaking her head.

"Uh, no, we are *not* eating that poor deer. Could you just let him go, please?"

Tez fought to keep a straight face as he complied with her wishes. He lifted the deer from his shoulders and placed both hands on its face. The deer immediately came to and got on its feet. Melanna walked slowly over to the deer. She let him sniff her hand and then she began to gently pet his head. When Melanna stopped petting the deer, it loped into the jungle unharmed. Manny was miffed that Tez seemed to be outdoing him on this outing. He turned his attention to cleaning the fish for cooking over the fire. Tez immediately caught the scent of the fish blood, which triggered his thirst. He excused himself, saying that he wanted to wash up at the stream. Melanna sat down beside Manny near the fire. He kept his eyes on the fish he was cooking on a spit over the fire.

"I feel like a fifth wheel here. Maybe after we eat, I should let you two continue on without me. I'm sure that my dad has loads of stuff for me to do at home anyway. I've been avoiding it. Besides, I see how Tez looks at you. He looks at you like you're a piece of meat!"

Melanna felt thrilled at this knowledge for a split second and then replied, "Is that so bad?"

"No, but if he does anything to hurt you, he'll have to answer to me!" He looked at her with one serious eye, the other hiding behind his hair.

"Don't worry. I'm certain that he's harmless."

"That's not what I meant, and you know that. I don't want him to toy with your heart. I want him to have good, honorable intentions."

Manny turned where he sat, faced Melanna, and put his hands on her arms as he continued.

"How well do you even know this guy? Is it even safe to leave you with him alone in the jungle? After all, you are not just anybody. You are *Princess* Melanna. But above all, you're one of my best friends."

After saying this, Manny put his arms around her and hugged her tightly to himself. Although Tez was quite a distance away, he could hear the conversation. He was glad that Melanna had a friend who was looking out for her. She reached over and put her hand on Manny's thigh.

"If you had only seen the way he handled a guy with a knife a couple of weeks ago, you wouldn't have to worry about him. The guy threatened to harm me. Tez broke his arm and put his lights out." She let that sink in before she went on. "I didn't want to hurt your feelings by not spending time with you today. You're still my best bud."

"Best bud of the non-female type?"

"Yes, my best buddy!"

And she planted a kiss on his cheek.

The fish were done in no time. Tez relaxed nearby. He claimed that he wasn't hungry. So Manny and Melanna shared both the fish and the food that she brought. It was one of the best breakfasts that Melanna ever had. It wasn't the food that made it memorable, but rather the company. Manny thanked them both for a good time then headed back home.

Once they were alone, Tez pulled a wooden flute from his pocket and began to play a remarkable tune. It seemed as though the creatures of the jungle were all mesmerized by the tune he played, as was Melanna. All inhabitants of the jungle both great and small became his audience. But Melanna didn't take notice of that. For her there was only him and for him there was only her just now, in this magical moment. Melanna took the opportunity to study the curves on Tez's face, the broadness of his shoulders, the sleek lines of his body, and the strong hands that held the flute to his lips. She wondered how those lips would feel on her own, if magical things would happen. She could have listened to him play for hours. But his song came to an end. Melanna clapped her hands in appreciation.

She stood and started walking over to Tez. Some movement on a high ridge on the other side of the stream caught Tez's attention. There was a man with a bow and arrow aimed at Melanna. Tez raced with lightening speed, seen only as a blur, to stand between her and the attacker. He got there faster than the arrow did and took the arrow in the back. He collapsed onto Melanna who crashed in horror to the ground beneath his weight. The attacker fled the scene even though he missed his mark. Tez winced in pain, but he stayed in control.

"Melanna, I need you to stay calm. Can you do that?" She nodded. Tears came to her eyes and she trembled. "Do you think that you could pull the arrow out?"

"I'll try. I've never done this before."

"I'm sure you'll do fine."

Tez rolled over and sat up. Melanna braced one foot on his back as she tried to pull out the arrow. She seemed to agonize at having to hurt him more to remove it. But finally the arrow came out. Tez collapsed once more, willing himself to rest a moment. His body healed quickly while he lay there unmoving with his eyes closed. He wondered to himself how he was going to explain away his recovery from this incident.

What am I going to do now? I really blew it this time. But I couldn't let her just die in front of me. I guess she was bound to find out the truth some time.

Melanna put the arrow on the ground beside her and lay close to his side. She placed her hand on his cheek and his forehead. He was so cold. Was it too late for him? Her mind raced. She needed to get help.

"Stay still and I will go get help for you."

As Melanna tried to spring into action, Tez grabbed her arm to stop her.

"What are you doing? Don't you understand that you may be dying? I need to get some help for you!"

Tez said nothing, but his eyes flew wide open and locked with hers. He slowly sat up. A chill went down Melanna's spine as she drew a sharp intake of breath. The hairs on the back of her neck stood up. One moment he looked like death and the next minute he appeared normal. Normal for him anyway.

In a quivering voice she said, "Let me see your back". He hesitated for a moment. "Please."

He pulled his shirt up nearly to his shoulders. Melanna placed her fingers where a large smear of blood marked the spot where the arrow was pulled from. The wound had closed up. Tez pulled his shirt back down.

"Okay. *This* is not normal!"

She stood on her feet, paced and thought about running from him. But she held her ground, turning to face him for some answers.

"I pulled that arrow from your back, and I know it went in deep so don't deny it. You've got a lot of explaining to do. We have the rest of the day and the jungle to ourselves. I'm waiting."

She folded her arms to her chest and stared at him expectantly.

10. TEZ'S SECRET REVEALED

Tez sat with his hands covering his face. They slowly slid down to his mouth as he gathered his thoughts. Where to begin? The beginning is always best. Why should he hide anything from her now? Especially considering that Zafrina was now taking over the kingdom and someone wanted Melanna dead.

"I'm not sure that you will like what I have to say."

"I just want the truth. I find myself drawn to you. I care about you. I feel something between us, and now - I'm afraid."

"Please don't be afraid. I have only meant to be there for you, to protect you. And I care very much for you too." He hesitated and looked with longing and tenderness into her eyes. "My story is an unusual one and not without its demons and its magic. I hope that I don't regret telling you everything."

Melanna nodded for him to go on. He retold the story of his past life when he had just gotten married. The bloodthirsty coven of vampires came upon him and his bride while they celebrated their nuptials. It was in the Northern Yucatan where there was a beautiful waterfall. The couple was scanning the coastline from above the waterfall, enjoying their beautiful surroundings when they came under attack. The Ancients quickly subdued them although Tez continued to fight them off. His bride lay dead on the shore. Tez stood on a huge boulder while their leader, Zafrina, gracefully pounced on him, moved his head to the side, and plunged her fangs into his neck. Before she completely drained him of blood, she stopped, tore her wrist open with her teeth, and forced him to drink her blood. Tez was dragged to the edge of the waterfall and was tossed over. This would have been the end for any normal man, but the blood from Zafrina in his body caused him to rise from the dead as a vampire.

Tez lay there cold and lifeless until night came. His body was in transition. He regained consciousness with his face partially submerged in water. There was a strange silver talisman dangling on his chest that hadn't been there before. His world had changed completely. He heard things his ears didn't used to hear and could see clearer than he used to see. Nighttime vision was as clear as the day to him. He could run faster and jump farther than the jaguar. He had the strength of several men. But he also burned with a great thirst. He thought he had gone mad, craving the blood of humans and animals alike. A small band of men from the Brotherhood of the Eagle were making a pilgrimage and discovered Tez in dirty rags, on the edge of sanity, and burning with the thirst. They said that they had encountered a few men like him in the past. They invited Tez to make the remaining journey with them to their temple.

That very night while his human companions slept, Tez succumbed to his new fallen nature. He moved with stealth in the dark from one victim to the next, plunging his fangs into their flesh and drinking with wild abandon. His last victim opened his eyes to look Tez squarely in the face and to address him in a clear voice.

"I forgive you and I love you, brother. Let the Great Spirit work in you."

The man's words trailed off, but with the last of his strength he pressed an eagle charm into the palm of Tez which seemed to brand his skin. Tez's hand closed over it into a fist and then dropped it to the floor. The brand glowed orange on his hand and slowly faded. With the blood of his victims on his face, he stood there in shock to hear those words spoken to him after he had done this heinous crime. The words seemed to be branded in his brain just like the eagle charm branded his flesh. They kept echoing over again. Soon angry cries of a mob pierced the darkness. With torches in hand, the humans came together as one to subdue the beast before them. Tez held his hands up in defense. The brotherhood immediately saw the brand in his hand and took it as a sign.

Tez spent several days locked away in a room. He was fed a steady diet of animal blood, not enough to satisfy, for he had tasted the sweetness and richness of human blood. None other would do. The animal blood was enough to keep him from going over the edge. Tez took an oath that he would not kill another human in the throes of self-indulgence to his fallen nature. He would honor the Great Spirit that way. His newfound faith made him stronger on the inside and filled him with hope. That took place nearly two hundred years ago.

Then his story lead to the day that Queen Almika gave birth to Melanna under the tree at Chichen Itza. Melanna let out a gasp, her eyes wide with shock at the mention of this. He further explained how he had made a promise to the queen to protect her baby girl, fulfilling that promise to the present day.

"You were mine to protect then. You are mine to protect even now. I have always been here for you even if you didn't realize it." He looked at her with longing, pleading eyes. Yet could she even look at him the same way after learning what kind of fallen creature he was?

Melanna stared at the ground with tears in her eyes and her hand over her mouth trying to take it all in. She closed her eyes and inhaled deeply. Now everything that she had seen and passed off as strange or just her imagination all made sense after his explanation: the swimming with the sharks, living alone inside a cenote, his brute strength, his ability to heal quickly, and his unearthly beauty.

She looked up at him and whispered, "But *what* are you?"

Tez closed his eyes. He took a deep breath and exhaled.

This is it.

He looked at her and said, "I am what is called a vampire, a child of the night. I am a 'day walker' because I wear this talisman around my neck. Otherwise, the sun's rays would burn me and I would become a pile of ash. I think that Zafrina placed it on me, hoping that I would join her afterwards. But I could never be a senseless killer that utterly destroys lives. I will never grow old and I cannot be destroyed easily. I will always be this." He spread his arms with his palms up to emphasize his statement. He tried to read her reaction. He took a few steps toward her and waited. A very long pause went by.

"You can trust me. You don't need to fear me."

Another long pause went by.

"Please say something."

Tez gave her a moment to deal with the information he just shared with her. He could see the turmoil going through her as her eyes looked about, filled with tears. She was falling for someone who has killed people, who could kill her now where she stands. But he has had so much taken away from him. He had no choice in his fate. Compassion filled her as she looked him square in the eyes as if trying to look into his soul.

"I know that I should be afraid, but you have saved my life twice now. Why should I be afraid of you?"

"Well, I am what I am and nothing will change that. I'm one of the world's most dangerous monsters that walk the earth, trying to cling to hope. I try to live this life so that it will count for something good. If I didn't have hope in the promise of the Great Spirit, I know for certain that I would truly go mad. I would give in to my cravings and be the most wretched of all creatures. And I would contribute to the damnation and destruction that Zafrina brings in her wake."

"I know that if you meant to bring me harm, you would've done it already. Surely you must still know what it feels like to be human, to love and care for people. All of that couldn't have left you because of what she did to you."

"It's not as simple as that. Death has a way of changing things. And this curse that I'm under, I feel like I'm barely hanging on sometimes. Like any moment I could erupt and the beast will come out. I'm really not safe to be around if you want to know the truth of it."

"I feel that I can trust you with my life. You make me feel safe, I can't explain it. As horrific as your story is, I can't picture my life without you." The words came from her lips almost involuntarily. Her eyes were tender at this admission.

Tez closed the gap between them and embraced her. His chin rested on her head. He placed a finger under her chin and tilted her face up to his and gently placed a kiss on her lips. Truly Melanna didn't know if she should fear this man that was embracing her and devouring her with his eyes. It was as if she had fallen under his spell, although Tez had not used compulsion on her. It was a different force that drew her to him like two magnets. Was it love? Was she too young to know what love is? Surely the giving of oneself, the selflessness to sacrifice your life for another, that had to be love. She had never in her life had encountered such love. And naturally she wanted to return those feelings.

"You know you don't look a day over twenty-three," she said with a faint smile, trying to lighten the moment.

"All the ladies tell me that," as he returned the smile.

Melanna took Tez's left hand and looked at the eagle brand in his palm.

She placed a kiss there and said, "If it weren't for this event, we most likely would've never met."

"Then I am doubly grateful that it happened, because I can't see living this life without you."

* * * * *

Melanna's attacker, Mulac, made his way back to the palace and he reported to Eleuia.

"Well, just don't stand there! Tell me what happened."

Mulac removed his helmet that had a face shield that concealed his face. A mass of black curly hair framed his face. He was a handsome young man with a lean muscular body, and he was one of the best guards in the palace when it came to handling a weapon. He certainly knew how to defend against enemies outside the palace; however, he easily succumbed to an enemy within.

"I followed them like you asked me to. I had your sister in my sight and took aim at her. Before the arrow reached her, the big guy stepped in front of her and took the arrow in his back."

"What! How could you make such a mistake! I've been told you're the best archer there is in the empire! I was grossly misguided."

"The man moved with such speed that he was there before I could strike my mark. I don't know if he survived or not. I didn't stick around to see."

"You mean you didn't finish the job and kill her?"

"No, I didn't!"

Mulac looked bewildered for a moment. Why would Eleuia want her sister dead so badly? Melanna was a likeable, beautiful, young woman. She was a peaceable person who wished no one ill.

"Look, if you want this done, you're going to have to get someone else to do it. I don't think I can. What do you have to gain from your sister's death anyway?" he said as he eyed her while drinking a goblet of wine.

Eleuia's face became hard as she said, "Don't let her façade of sweetness cloud your judgment. She will bring Zafrina's wrath upon us if she tries to join the resistance. And there is only room in the palace for one heir to the throne. So spare me any reservations you may have about my sister and concentrate on the task at hand."

Eleuia tried another approach as she poured on her charm. She came closer to Mulac and placed a caressing hand on well-muscled arm.

"Listen, lover, we can discuss this later. Tomorrow is another day. There is no rush. I say that we go find a party to crash tonight," she said as she planted a warm, seductive kiss on him.

11. ZAFRINA'S INVITATION

That same day as an attempt was made on Melanna's life, Noctli spied a group of dark clad people wearing masks, known as the Ancients, rounding up victims for the evening's sacrificial ceremony. The victims were not criminals, in fact Noctli remembered seeing a few of them speak out against Zafrina in public. He quickly realized that something terrible was in store for these people. Noctli rushed over to try to stop what was happening. He jumped on the back of one of the Ancients while his hands continued to find something to cling to. The mask fell away from the face of the old vampire. Noctli fell to the ground and looked into the face of the monster. A sick feeling of shock and dread overcame him as he stared at the pus colored, wrinkled face of the old vampire who was baring his fangs at him. Noctli couldn't will himself to move, but found himself subdued quickly by the Ancients too.

"You won't get away with this! I am a friend of Princess Melanna! She will see the injustice of what you are doing."

He was quickly gagged and bound. A feeling of horror spread through him when he realized that there was no escape for any of them.

Sunset was near. The crowd gathered at the foot of the pyramid. The Ancients accompanied Nocli to the sacrificial alter. He had been compelled by the Dark One to give himself without resistance, and so he did with a smile of wild anticipation. Zafrina started the ceremonial chant followed with the Ancients repeating after her. The crowd was pulled in to the excitement and hysteria of the sacrifice. Her knife plunged into his chest, ripping out his heart. And then it was over, but not for the hungry vampires waiting for their leader to join them as they planned to feast on the blood of the remaining victims that were abducted earlier.

Melanna and her friends were crushed. They clung to each other crying and trying to comfort one another while the rest of the onlookers went their way into the city to carry on as normal. Melanna confronted her father, King Tetaneeka, about her friend being unjustly killed. The king tried to quell the chilling fear in his heart by cowering in the beautiful lush gardens of his palace. Tetaneeka chose to submit to Zafrina's wishes rather than risk crossing her. Melanna took a stand, although she felt alone in her choice. There would be no justice this evening for Noctli. But Melanna vowed in her heart that she would do everything in her power to rid the city of the murderous cult that had taken over.

Zafrina's spy who had witnessed the exchange between the king and Melanna made his way back to Zafrina's chamber. After being told the details of the conversation, her wrath was ignited as she growled and bore her fangs. She managed to regain a cool composer as she came up with a solution just as quickly as her anger had flared. She summoned a very close confidant who resided in another chamber of the pyramid. Moments later, her guard stood on either side of the handsome vampire as he was announced.

"Lord Chak Kojolaxel."

Zafrina gave a dismissive nod to the guards who left the two alone in the chamber.

"To what do I owe the pleasure of your company, my dark and alluring queen?" With the grace of a jungle cat, Chak walked slowly into Zafrina's chamber. He was dressed in a black shirt that was opened to reveal a sleek, creamy, muscular body. His black pants, which were made of the same black gauzy material, were worn low on his hips, accentuating the length of his torso. His hair was chestnut brown, wavy and shoulder length. His looks were to die for.

"I'm sure that you are familiar with the king of this city? King Tetaneeka?"

Chak rolled his eyes as he commented on the boring subject, "If you mean the old man in the palace who has poor taste in style and eats and drinks like a pig, such a waste of space. Yes, I'm familiar with him."

"I do not see him as hindering our plans for this city, but his daughter, Melanna, could be a potential problem for us. My spy just returned with news of a conversation between the king and his daughter. There may be a little uprising if she has her way."

"We've handled many uprisings over the centuries. She is nothing."

Zafrina's head snapped in the direction of Chak. "Don't underestimate this problem for a minute. I have an idea, and I would like to know if you'll go along with me on this."

"I'm at your service, my queen. I will do anything in my power to honor you and give you pleasure."

He walked and stood behind her. Chak placed his hand on Zafrina's shoulder along with a kiss. His hand glided down to the center of her back with an intimate lover's touch.

"As you know in times past that when two kingdoms want to be united, that a marriage between royalties will bring unity."

"Yes, but what part do you want me to play in this?"

Zafrina turned in Chak's embrace to face him. Her fingers stroked the back of his head. Her eyes met his.

A hint of a smile played on her lips as she said, "I want you to marry princess Melanna."

Chak's eyes twinkled with evil delight as he smiled back at his dark queen.

"Anything to please you, my queen. You will have to make the arrangements of course. I'll leave everything in your capable hands."

Chak's lips left a trail of kisses under her collarbone as he pressed her to his body.

"All in good time, my conquering prince."

* * * * *

The next day a messenger appeared at the palace asking for King Tetaneeka. The king appeared in the great hall to receive the messenger's invitation. And thus the message read:

> *If it please your majesty to attend a dinner this evening in your family's honor. Dinner will be served at the small Banquet Hall. We would like to discuss events that would be beneficial to the kingdom and to the future of the great city of Coba. Please send your R.S.V.P. back with the messenger.*
>
> *~ Zafrina*

It looked like the letter was stamped with a signet ring by Zafrina. King Tetaneeka told the messenger that he and his two daughters would attend the dinner. The messenger bowed to the king and then left the palace to report to Zafrina.

The small Banquet Hall was in fact an abandoned temple. The architecture and location appealed to Zafrina. It was situated at the edge of the jungle, away from the goings on of the city. A meandering, low-lying stairways lead to a plain white building. That is "plain" except for its tall, showy archway in the front. Zafrina's artisans worked on the interior of the building until it contained as much gold and pomp as her own dwellings, suitable for royalty. She sent another messenger to the palace to inquire of the cook about the favorite dishes that the royal family enjoyed best.

The king, Melanna and Eleuia arrived at the Banquet Hall a couple of hours before sunset. They were greeted by scantily clad female servants who wore silken, deep v-cut bodices that nearly went to their belly buttons. One was awestruck to look at their faces because they were so beautiful and flawless. They did their duties without a hint of emotion, like dark angels fulfilling the wishes of a higher power. The king and his daughters lounged in a grand foyer before the meal was served. The girls busied themselves with studying the various pieces that adorned the walls. None of the artifacts looked like they came from the local region. Of course not! Zafrina traveled the world in her quest for domination and destruction. Collecting memorabilia was just something she did on the side to remind her of the civilizations that she conquered. Someday there would be something from Coba to add to her collection.

Zafrina and Chak entered the foyer and greeted them. Chak gave the king a deep bow, and then he took the hand of Eleuia and next Melanna and kissed it in greeting. When he came to Melanna, he could sense her purity and shyness. This only aroused the beast in him to want to corrupt everything that was good in her. His look was smoldering which made her uneasy. She turned away. It was like looking into the face of an unblinking snake.

Zafrina announced that dinner was ready. They all walked into the dining area and gave an appraising look at the table which was laid out with bowls of local fruit, wine, exotic flowers, and formal service ware. The king sat at one end and Zafrina sat at the other end. The two young women sat across from Chak. When the food was served, the plates of Zafrina and Chak were left untouched throughout the meal. But they did manage to ask for refills of red "wine". The king and his daughters thoroughly enjoyed their meals. The conversation was guarded around the table. Eleuia stole many hungry glances at Chak across the table. She wondered how he had escaped her endless search for a boy-toy, an object of her run away desires.

Zafrina thought it was time to broach the subjects at hand.

"So, your majesty, tell me your feelings about the direction of your city of Coba. Do you think that your people as a whole are accepting of the Way of Sacrifice that we've brought to your kingdom? After all, you are having an abundant crop, the rain is plentiful, and the cattle are flourishing. The people seem to enjoy the sacrificial festivities too, and participate freely."

Tetaneeka was uncomfortable discussing this subject with her, but had no choice in the matter. He only allowed these things to go on because of his own fear.

"Most of the people seem to accept this; however, there are a few who resist."

Melanna's heartbeat quickened and she looked down at the table. Zafrina and Chak could hear the change of her heart in the pause of the conversation and exchanged a look between themselves. The king went on.

"I am not sure if that could present a problem in the near future or not. There are many patriotic people who will not stand by to see close friends being sacrificed without a good reason."

Melanna sank a little in her chair.

Zafrina looked mildly miffed as she said, "My apologies. I didn't know that we were slaying innocent blood. The Ancients have been instructed to take only criminals to be sacrificed. This has not come to my attention before now. Do you happen to know of any such victims?"

Melanna could not restrain her tongue at such a blatant lie.

With a fist on the table she said in a firm voice, "You just sacrificed Noctli last night! How could you *not* know that he was innocent of any crime? How many other people have you grabbed off the street to put in your religious side show?"

Zafrina seethed inside but held her composure well. Eleuia looked amused at the reaction of her sister. Chak looked on without emotion.

Tetaneeka said, "You must forgive my daughter. Noctli's death has been hard on her and her friends. I apologize for her rudeness."

"Rude?" Melanna's eyes bugged out at her father's response and her outrage was cut short by Zafrina.

"Apology accepted. And I'm sure that we will investigate this matter further," Zafrina said with a nod, "which comes to my next topic of discussion. I think that it is in your best interest and the interest of your kingdom, that one of your daughters gives her hand in marriage to a colleague of mine, thus having your seal of approval. This will ensure your way of life is preserved. It will ensure our place beside you in your kingdom. And peace will abide in your city." Zafrina sat with her elbows on the table, folded her hands, and rested her chin on top of them. She waited for the king to respond.

Melanna interrupted once more, "Please, father, you can't allow these people to just march in here and take over everything and diminish your power! Please do something!"

"Quiet, child! Or I'll have you sent to another room in order for us to continue without interruption!"

"No need for that, your majesty. In fact, this concerns her too. Please continue," Zafrina offered.

"Has someone come forth asking to wed one of my daughters?"

"Yes, and that person just happens to be Lord Chak." Zafrina reached out her hand in the direction of where Chak was seated.

Chak addressed the king saying, "Your majesty, I would like to ask for Melanna's hand in marriage."

A gasp escaped both daughters at his proposal. Eleuia was both miffed and aghast that Chak should prefer Melanna to her.

What a ridiculous choice! If he could only know how I could pleasure a man! Really, what was he thinking? That bore of a sister will never be woman enough for him.

Tetaneeka was mildly taken aback. But given the circumstances, he wanted to comply with everything that Zafrina wanted. His thoughts were only for his own preservation and the preservation of his kingdom. His daughter did not come first in his love or his priorities. His heart once again visited those feelings of blame for the death of his precious Queen Almika. What better way to assuage some of that pain than to marry off his daughter to this stranger?

"This truly comes as a surprise." He laughed, but it sounded hollow. "I give you my approval and my blessing." Both young women turned to look at their father: Eleuia out of bitter envy; Melanna out of betrayal.

Melanna's heartbeat once again betrayed her feelings as it sped up. The blood rushed to her face. Her jugular vein popped out on her neck. Chack eyed her with such thirst that his fangs started to extend and caused him to salivate. Zafrina mirrored those feelings as well.

"Father, how could you agree to this? We don't even know this man! Don't you care about my happiness?" Melanna's eyes overflowed with tears at her supplication. "Do I mean so little to you that you would give me away?"

"It has been an old Mayan tradition to make arranged marriages. We've made an agreement, daughter. I am your father *and* your king. You *will* submit to my will and that of your future husband. I will hear no more on the matter."

Treating Melanna in this manner ensured that he would not incur Zafrina's wrath. He saw no other way to accomplish this.

Chak breathed deeply to control his urges and said, "It is my honor to enter into a marriage contract with you, Melanna." She glanced unwillingly at those unfeeling snake eyes that repulsed her. "I promise to fulfill it in every way." His eyes raked over her body in unabashed lust. "Everyone will benefit from our marriage. You will surely come to see that."

Zafrina clapped her hands together and said, "Good! I hope that this arrangement unites us as we look forward to the future together! I think a toast is in order."

Everyone raised their glasses except for Melanna who sat in her chair, stunned at the turn of events. She was more stunned at her father's response than she was about the marriage proposal. Did she truly mean so little to him that he cared nothing for what she felt? His own flesh and blood? She felt as though a dagger were thrust into her heart.

As they made merry around the table, Melanna rose from her seat and ran out of the Banquet Hall. The wind whipped at her hair and her tears. Thankfully, night had fallen. No one could recognize her. She ran hard and fast into the night, ignoring the burning in her lungs. Her pace slowed and she walked the back streets of the city. Melanna just wanted to melt into the darkness and forget that this terrible night ever happened.

12. THE RESISTANCE REVEALED

Melanna walked by a temple that she never noticed before. It had a crest of a dancing eagle above the door similar to the one on Tez's cuff bracelets. On both sides of the entrance there were well-manicured shrubs and a blazing Eternal Torch to welcome all people at any time. Melanna entered the temple to find it illuminated by hundreds of candles. A priest of the brotherhood was at the front of the temple, offering up prayers. Upon hearing Melanna's footsteps, the man rose from the altar to greet her.

"Princess Melanna! It's so good to see you. Tez has told me so much about you. My name is Amoxtli," he said as he extended his hand in greeting.

As Melanna came closer and took his hand, Amoxtli could see her swollen eyes and sad expression.

"I'm sorry. Is there something I can do to help you?"

"I just came from the Banquet Hall where my father and sister still dine with Zafrina. We were asked there so that I could be promised in marriage to her closest confidant named Chak." The tears flowed freely after having shared this with him.

Being a man of faith and in a position that he counseled the public, he embraced her and tried to sooth her worries away. But a frown furrowed his brow because he knew in fact that Tez loved Melanna with all his heart. He knew that trouble was coming. And Amoxtli also knew that Zafrina and her ilk were the most evil vampires spawned from the pit of hell.

"Do not be so utterly cast down, child. Have faith that the Great Spirit will act on your behalf. Won't you pray with me? I guarantee that it will lift your spirit."

Amoxtli lit yet another candle before kneeling at the altar. Melanna joined him there and closed her eyes. She began to weep and groan. Amoxtli began entreating the Great Spirit out loud with his arms lifted and his palms up. There was a rush of wind that made the hundreds of candles flicker. Amoxtli continued to entreat the Great Spirit. The flames from every candle suddenly lengthened a little higher, then abated. Then the smoke from the candles gathered in one intentional direction and entered Melanna's body through her nose and mouth. Her eyes flew open as if she had just witnessed a revelation. Her heart was at peace. It was as if a great burden had been lifted from her.

"My child, did I not say that He would lift your spirit? He has indeed because I can see the difference on your face."

Melanna was in awe that her fear and sadness were gone. Words could not describe what she was feeling. All she knew is that she felt much lighter inside as if a great burden had been lifted. She reached for Amoxtli and threw her arms around him for joy.

"Wait. I would like to give something to you to remember this moment."

He reached on the other side of the altar and picked up a box. In it were cuff bracelets. He chose a petite cuff bracelet with a medallion of the dancing eagle on it. She gladly accepted his gift and immediately put it on. She now had something in common with Tez.

And speaking of Tez, where is he tonight?

"Before you go, I would like to show you around the temple if you don't mind."

Amoxtli took Melanna with her hand in the crook of his arm and lead her to the different artifacts passed down through the ages of the Brotherhood of the Eagle. These consisted of hand written parchments of words inspired by the Great Spirit. There were very old cups and utensils that were passed down from the very first temple that were hundreds of years old. A very large and ancient book lay near these. It looked worn and faded, having been passed down from one generation to the next. The title was "The Fall of Man & the Promise of the Great Spirit". Melanna lingered there, staring at the book. Amoxtli assured her that there would be a better time for her to see it later since it was getting late. She looked up to see a Mayan style ancient stone relief carving which was displayed on the wall depicting the likeness of the founder of the faith with the words chiseled below it "His spirit soars with the eagles for eternity". Melanna placed her fingers on the carving and felt its rough raised edges. There was a very regal silver helmet trimmed in Mayan blue sitting on a shelf.

"What is so special about this helmet?"

"According to traditions that have been passed down through generations, the wearer of this helmet is immune to the magical powers of the elements conjured up by evil forces. It is literally the helmet of salvation." He paused and then he prodded her memory by saying, "Remember Bonfire Night?"

"Do I ever! People will be talking about that for a long time!"

"Well, say if you were wearing this helmet about the time that the hail and fire fell from the sky. This helmet acts as an umbrella to the forces that may come against you by the Dark One."

Next to the helmet were a shield and sword done in the same beautiful Mayan blue and silver.

"Are these 'gifted' weapons too?"

"The shield is guaranteed to stop any type of arrow: flaming, metal, obsidian or otherwise. And the wielder of the sword receives spiritual discernment from the Great Spirit. Also the one who wields the sword is always the victor over his enemy. It holds great power in battle."

Completing the set of armor was a silver breastplate adorned with a large dancing eagle.

Then they at last came to a bone dagger that had intricate carvings of sacred scriptures and symbols on it. It rested on top of an ornate stone box that contained the ashes of departed brothers of the faith.

"And this is our most prized possession. This is the Dagger of Qajawaxal. It was made from the leg bone of a holy man of the brotherhood who hunted vampires. It has been blessed and commissioned by the brotherhood. It deals a death blow to vampires when it is plunged in their heart."

Melanna stopped dead in her tracks.

"Vampires? Do you believe they exist?"

She was testing the waters here because she didn't know who to trust with Tez's secret.

"You don't need to be coy with me, Melanna. I know all about Tez. In fact I know all about Zafrina and those demonic creatures, the Ancients, which live in that pyramid with her. Tez, although tragically turned by Zafrina centuries ago, now lives by the faith of the brotherhood. He *is* one of us. But Zafrina and her kind are a deathly cancer to this kingdom and must be stopped. It is written in our prophecy,

'She who is pure of heart and noble birth shall smite the devil queen whose reign will come to an end and whose kingdom will be utterly destroyed. Peace will rule the land thereafter.'"

"Wow, it can't happen soon enough!"

"Maybe you have a part to play in all this, who knows?" he said as he studied her. "The Great Spirit uses people great and small to do His work."

"I'm so young and just out of school. How can I be used in any big way to change the world? You know, just look at me!" she said as she gestured with her gaze at the length of her and her arms outstretched.

"In your weakness, the Great Spirit is strong! Don't ever forget that."

"I suppose I should be getting back to the palace. At least Qaileen will have missed me if no one else did. If Tez should come by here, will you tell him that I visited you and to come see me?"

"Of course I will, princess." He clasped her hand and kissed it, sending her home for the evening.

* * * * *

Tez did not follow Melanna to the Temple of the Brotherhood of the Eagle because he remained outside of the Banquet Hall to listen to the conversations taking place inside. Since the building was situated on the edge of the jungle, Tez had a front row seat in the trees. His heart constricted within him as Melanna tried her best to make her father listen to reason. Then he experienced a deep jealousy with the intensity of a vampire, much stronger than a human emotion, when Chak made his proposal of marriage for Melanna. He wanted to snap right there and then, but he held his composure. Every fiber of his being cried out when Melanna ran from the Banquet Hall. But Tez remained in control to learn more. Pleasantries were exchanged. The merry making went on a little longer until Tetaneeka and Eleuia were bid good night. When the guests were gone, Zafrina and Chak lounged at the table to finish their blood meal for the night.

"That little tramp really gets under my skin for some reason," Zafrina's eye's rolled.

"Yes, Eleuia is just that! And she doesn't even try to hide it!"

"I was talking about your bride to be." She smiled with amusement at him and the corners of his mouth turned up a bit too. Wanting to wrap things up she continued, "So we'll have the wedding a month from now. The moon will be at its fullest so that I may draw more Power from it. That should also give us time to rid ourselves of more of the resistance that are in hiding before our little lamb is brought to slaughter."

"Of course! Just say the word and it will be done, my queen."

"Just remember that on your wedding night, Melanna will succumb to a terrible accident which results in her death. We can blame it on wild animals or something. Be creative. Between the two of us we'll think of something believable. We'll stop the resistance one victim at a time."

"Don't worry. After I'm wed to the princess and I'm finally alone with her, she's as good as dead. But, of course, not before I've derived some satisfaction on my wedding night."

Zafrina flashed her evil, sensual smile as she placed her hand on his cheek and said teasingly, "I love it when you're such a beast! You're so hot!"

Melanna got hardly any sleep at all that evening. Images of that seductive, beautiful face with the look of an unblinking snake haunted her mind all night long. For a fact, she could never love him. Tez was the one she loved.

* * * * *

The next morning Melanna decided to take a walk into the city to her favorite park to meditate for a while in the beautiful gardens. There's nothing like the beauty of nature to sooth the troubled spirit. On the way there, she happened to meet up with Manny. He seemed excited about something, and he was just itching to talk to her. He caught up with her and walked her pace as he put an arm around her head to bring it close to him for a hug. He greeted her with a smile and she gazed into his deep brown eye that wasn't covered by his shiny straight hair.

"Hi, beautiful! You don't look your perky self today. What's up?"

"It's so awful!" She bit her lip and shook her head. "I can't begin to tell you how I'm feeling right now. I feel like my own father has betrayed me!" Her eyes welled up with tears.

"What? Please, tell me what happened."

"Zafrina invited my father, Eleuia and me to a formal dinner. It was there that Chak, an associate of Zafrina's, proposed marriage to me. Zafrina promised harmony and prosperity in the kingdom if this happened. Of course, my father was all for this. It was as if I was traded like some commodity or something. I had no say in the matter." Melanna placed her hand over her forehead as she continued to fret and cry, "I feel like I'm being thrown away. How can my own father do this to me?"

With this knowledge, it both frightened and angered Manny and he tensed his jaw and he stared at the ground while focusing on nothing. He knew how evil and controlling Zafrina was. He also knew how uncaring Tetaneeka was to his daughter. But this was very low. There could be nothing good to come out of this union. Manny stopped walking and stood there conflicted with his emotions after learning this. But fear melted as anger brewed stronger within him. He grabbed Melanna in a hug to sooth her sadness and whispered in her ear that everything would be okay. After a moment, Manny flung his hair back from his face, took her by the hand and they continued to walk.

After entering the park, Melanna sat on the grass close to a lake and watched Manny as he took his anger out by hurling stones into the water. And finally he decided to tell Melanna what was on his mind. Manny sat on the grass next to her and spoke in low tones.

"You *do* know that Zafrina and her bunch pretty much control things around here, right?"

"Yes, I've known that for a little while now. My father is too afraid to do anything to oppose her, which includes refusing to give my hand in marriage to that man."

"What I'm about to tell you, I don't want you repeating to anyone. Deal?"

"Yes, deal."

"There is a large faction of combatants who oppose what Zafrina is doing to our city. They have been waiting for the right time to take action since your father doesn't seem to have the stomach for such things."

"How can anyone go up against a force like hers? You've seen what she can do! She has power over the very elements of this world. And she has a small army to do her bidding."

"Everyone has a weakness. I don't believe that Zafrina is indestructible. And I also don't believe that evil ultimately overcomes good."

Manny happened to glance down at the new bracelet of the dancing eagle that Melanna was wearing. "Nice bracelet. Where did you get it?"

"I was walking by the Temple of the Brotherhood of the Eagle last night. I met an interesting man named Amoxtli there. He gave it to me," she said as she ran her fingers over the shiny petite cuff bracelet. "He shared some very odd but interesting things with me."

"Such as?"

"Such as all of the very old and magical artifacts that are displayed in the temple. He sounded to me as if he may have a part in defeating Zafrina too. He even quoted an ancient prophecy about a girl of a pure heart and noble birth striking a blow against the devil queen, or something like that. Imagine that! The kingdom being saved by a girl! Do you think that's bull feathers or is there any truth in it?" Her eyebrows pinched together as her mouth formed a smirk at her own question.

"I think that all things are possible, especially where the Great Spirit is concerned." He looked at her out of the corner of his eye and went on, "Yes, I know about the temple. I was drawn there myself out of grief after the death of Noctli. I was filled with so much hate that it eclipsed every good thing inside of me. It was consuming me. Then I met Amoxtli. I left there a changed person and with a new resolve that I would be a part of defeating those blood suckers."

"Exactly what do you mean by that?"

Melanna had never known Manny to give himself for a cause until now. Manny was somewhere between a man and a boy as far as physical and mental maturity was concerned, but this was a very serious matter.

He swiped his slick hair back from his face as he said, "I vowed that I would join the resistance and do whatever I can to put an end to the evil that has taken over our city. I have been training with some members of the brotherhood for special combat. Not only that, but I found out what kind of monsters those things really are. They are not some wicked 'cult' as some have said they are. They are vampires, immortals that can't be easily killed." Manny paused to look into the eyes of Melanna. "No one really knows where they came from or how old they are. They've been around for a very long time, that is, accordingly to Amoxtli."

A chill went down Melanna's spine as she heard the words coming from her friend. She took a moment to do a mental comparison of Tez to the wicked vampires that Manny was describing. How could one vampire be so loving and caring while another did nothing but spread death and destruction? And the only conclusion that came to her was that vampires had free will too. How could Tez be the same creature? But yet, humans can be so vastly different from one another too, like night and day, evil versus good, or brutality versus nurturing.

"So now you are convinced that they are vampires? Do you really believe that?" Melanna tested her friend's conviction on the matter.

"I believe that they have conquered many nations that were seduced in every way by them. They are trying to do the same here. They will destroy everything and everyone that we hold dear. And when they are finished, they'll move on to another unfortunate city or kingdom to suck it dry too. They are nothing but the worse kind of parasites that could have ever existed! But if we rise up and say, 'Enough is enough,' and take the fight to them, I think that we have a chance of our survival."

"What makes you think that we have a fighting chance against these vampires?"

"Because we have people that have experience in dealing with this vermin. I also believe in the prophecy too, that a woman warrior will lead us in our quest for freedom. The only one besides your sister with noble blood around here is you." Melanna looked intently into Manny's eyes as he said, "So if I were you, I'd do a lot of soul searching right now."

"Even if it were true, do you know how big of a burden that would be on me to lead our people to freedom against Zafrina? And look at me! Do I look like warrior material to you? When have you ever known me to pick up any weapon let alone face an army?"

"No, I know that you've never taken an interest in acquiring fighting skills. You'd rather be shopping and doing girlie stuff. But that doesn't mean that you wouldn't be good at it." He paused for a moment and then said, "Why don't you come with me tomorrow morning to the training camp. I'll introduce you to some people. The least you could do is observe. But the survival of our people depends on your actions."

"Well, since you put it that way, I do have a responsibility, even if my father fails to do anything. What kind of princess would I be if I let my people down, right?"

They both stood up and began to walk around the lake at a slow pace.

"I'll go with you tomorrow. How about we meet here in the morning and you can take me there?"

"Okay. Tomorrow it is. Wear something that you don't mind getting dirty or ripped."

Manny and Melanna parted ways. She lingered in the park to meditate on what she had just talked about with Manny. She knew that eventually she would have to tell her friends about the wedding that her father arranged for her. Melanna knew what their reactions would be before she even told them. She made her way to Nelli's house who was home helping her mother prepare a meal.

"Hey, Mel, it's about time that you showed your face around here. But I can tell that something is bothering you."

"Yes, something *really is* bothering me." She remembered that she couldn't talk about what Manny had shared with her. She wanted all of her friends present at the same time to tell them about the arranged marriage.

"Do you mind if we walk to meet Zonya and Teela? I have something important to share with all of you."

"Sure! Let me tell my mother that I'm leaving with you."

They walked to Zonya's house where she and Teela were lounging on large pillows in the over sized living area of the house. They just happened to be discussing which of their friends had found their life mate and planned to wed soon.

After a short interval, Melanna said, "I know a couple that will be married soon."

All of them piped up, "Who? Tell us."

"I um...," she tried to force the words out, "I am to marry Lord Chak"

The girls just sat there like it didn't register in their brains and then they broke out in hysteric laughter.

Zonya said, "Stop with the jokes, ok, Melanna?!"

"I wish it were a joke!" Melanna had tears well up in her eyes as she hugged herself for security.

Her friends immediately flocked around her for support. Their demeanor immediately changed at the realization of the sobering truth.

"I am so hurt that my father made an arranged marriage to Zafrina's colleague, Chak, even though my father knows I don't want this. He agreed to it because he's afraid of her."

Nelli tried to look at the bright side by saying, "It *is* tradition to do an arranged marriage here in Coba. Our people have been doing it for hundreds of years. After having a few children, things will be as they've always been for you. The only thing you should be worried about is what you'll be wearing to the ceremony."

Nelli said this with good intentions. Her friends still didn't know that these undead usurpers were vampires bent on the destruction of their people. To them, this news was just the natural goings on of the kingdom, an arranged marriage and the continuation of the royal family.

"Something inside of me tells me it won't work out that way," Melanna said as she bit her lip.

"Did you really expect to be able to plan who you would marry since you *are* the king's daughter? And he is doing the only thing he knows how at the moment to keep the peace. You can't blame him for that," said Teela.

"You weren't there! You didn't see how he forced it against my will. You also weren't there to see me running from the Banquet Hall."

Zonya reasoned, "Surely it can't be all that bad. What does this Chak guy look like anyway? And would *we* like him?"

"He is the most perfect looking man you could ever lay eyes on. *He's too perfect.* It's as if he existed to be worshiped by women. And he looks at me like his next meal, like he's going to pounce on me."

Nelli smiled and said, "Well, there's nothing wrong with that!"

"There's more. It's as if evil radiates from him. He stares at me like a calculating, unblinking snake. And I have no doubt that his touch would be the same way too."

"Maybe this is all in your head since your father has decreed that you should marry him. Maybe you are just resentful about it right now. That and your lack of experience with the opposite sex are making you cynical," Nelli shrugged.

The other two nodded their heads. But Nelli regretted her words as soon as she had spoken them.

Incredulously Melanna said, "How could you even think that, when he is a close associate of Zafrina's? Or have you forgotten how she murdered Noctli just days ago?"

Nelli hung her head. "You have a point there. I'm sorry for my attitude just now. I want you to be happy, but I agree that this is asking too much of you," she said as she gave Melanna an affectionate hug.

Melanna looked angry and sad as she said, "And the worst part of this is that I love someone else while I'm being forced into this marriage."

Her girlfriends looked at one another in shock at this revelation. They stood up and embraced each another in a group hug. Tears flowed and they comforted one another saying that it would all work out somehow. But would it really?

13. TRAINING DAY BEGINS

Melanna met Manny as planned early in the morning. They walked the back streets and made their way to the outskirts of the city. They walked a winding path to what looked like an old shack at the edge of the jungle that looked like it was about to be swallowed up by the plush growth. Manny gave two knocks at the door. A big burly man peeked through the small window of the door to identify who was there.

"What is *she* doing here?" he said in a gruff voice.

"She needs to be here! She is the one that the prophecy has foretold according to Amoxtli."

"We'll see about that!" And the old door creaked open to let them in.

The room was very dim and very small. All three of them crossed the room in a few strides to the door on the other side. The burly man opened the door for them as sunlight spilled into the room. The jungle was cleared away making room for an informal training camp, which was full of people paired off doing drills with swords and other weapons. About halfway down the field to the left and lounging in the shade was Amoxtli. He was both a supervisor and a weapons depot to the resistance. He yelled instructions to some who were yet a little slow in countering their opponents.

"So he does get out of the temple occasionally," Melanna said to Manny, and they both smiled. They joined Amoxtli on the sidelines.

"It is great to see you here, princess. Have you come to satisfy your curiosity or perhaps to take an active role?"

"Both I guess. I feel it is my duty to defend my city, sir."

"Are you prepared to give your life for our cause? This is no small thing that we're doing. You do realize that, don't you? This is life or death."

"Yes, I understand and I want to be a part of it. For me there is no going back."

"Good, how soon do you want to get started?"

"I guess the sooner the better."

Amoxtli lead Melanna to a table of weapons to see what she should start out with. Melanna was drawn to a dagger that was embellished with gold and jewels. But she eventually chose a plainer, heftier, and sharper one.

"Good choice, Melanna! I don't think that gold one could've cut butter." He smiled with his hand over his mouth as if she had passed a test.

"I would like you to spar with the dagger in your left hand while you wield a sword in your right hand. Do you think that you can handle this?"

"Why do I need two weapons at the same time?"

"The dagger is good for fending off another blade and for using at a closer range. It complements the use of the sword."

"Whatever you think is best," she said with a shrug.

They walked over to a second table that had different styles of swords. She chose a sword that wasn't too cumbersome for her to practice with if it were used for a prolonged period.

Amoxtli walked her over to a female who had been resting and drinking water after having already fenced with someone.

"Melanna, this is Xoco. Xoco this is Princess-"

"Ya, I know who she is. No introduction needed," she said as she gave Melanna a firm handshake as they locked eyes in a guarded stare.

Xoco could have passed as a sister to Melanna with her jet black hair and dark eyes except that her look could change from one of joy to one of severity: for example I-won't-take-any-of-your-crap kind of looks. She looked much more tomboyish too, like she was one of the guys.

"Nice to meet you, Melanna. I'm glad you're here. We need all the help that we can get."

"It's nice to meet you too. How long have you been with the resistance?"

"The resistance formed almost overnight after Zafrina and her cronies took over the city. I knew that I had to do something so I joined immediately. I don't have extraordinary fighting skills. It's just that I come from a family with many boys and I'm the only girl. You might say that it prepared me a little for this."

"I can imagine," Melanna said with a smile. "It would be nice if you could show me some basic moves. I don't have any experience at all."

"Sure! Just try to keep up. If I need to, I'll tell you where to place your feet and how you should have countered. Ready?"

"Yes!"

They walked out into the open and took a fighting stance. Melanna held her dagger with the handle pointing upward which was good for blocking and stabbing. She held her sword in a defensive posture. Xoco did likewise with her weapons. They fenced for two hours while Melanna became better with handling her weapons. Xoco was an excellent teacher. She admired Melanna for taking an active part in fighting against their common enemy. They took a short break as they hydrated themselves with cool water under the shade trees.

"You're very good, Xoco! What's your secret? Do you sleep with those things?"

"No, of course not. I only sleep with my dagger," she said with a grin. Melanna knew that she meant it as she smiled and shook her head.

Manny walked over to the two, all sweaty from his training. He poured himself some water and then dumped it on his face and down his chest. And then he drank a cup full.

"How 'bout it, Mel? You want to go a few rounds with me on the field?"

"No, I'd rather watch for a little while and catch my breath. But maybe Xoco is up for it."

Xoco had admired Manny for a while but never approached him. She quickly took advantage of the moment.

"I've seen you train her before, but we've never been introduced. I'm Xoco. And you are?" She extended her hand in greeting.

Manny grabbed her hand and gave it a lazy shake. He tried to brush his hair back from his face with his fingers, but it fell again to cover half of his face. He addressed her with one appraising brown eye.

"I'm Manauia but my friends call me Manny. Glad to meet you."

"Are you up for some more fencing?"

Manny wanted to "man up" in front of the ladies, so naturally he said, "Why not? You want to make this fun? Like, the winner gets something in return?"

Xoco tapped her temple with her index finger and said, "Okay, what are the terms?"

"We fight until the other relents at the point of a sword."

"Are there any rules at all?"

"None."

"Okay, if I win, I get to give you a haircut," Xoco said as she unsmilingly cocked her head to the side while meeting his gaze.

Manny pondered that for a moment.

"And if I win, I get to kiss you," Manny said with a little bit of arrogance.

Xoco seemed neither surprised nor unwilling to accept this.

"Okay, you're on," she said with her chin jutting out defiantly.

They walked out to the field near the center. Others stopped their training to watch the two of them fight. Manny and Xoco took their positions and then it started. Xoco took a challenging swing at Manny with more force than he had anticipated. He almost dropped his sword. A stunned look crossed his face, which quickly changed to him baring his teeth and wrinkling his nose. He decided that if she wanted to play rough, he could play rough too. They came at each other with swords chopping the air and the sound of steel on steel, whipping and whirling, in a type of graceful dance. The men in the field hooped and hollered as they cheered the two on. Manny swung his sword low while Xoco jumped to avoid the blow. Likewise, Xoco swung her sword to bring a head blow to Manny while he effortlessly blocked it. They kept this up for a full fifteen minutes. Finally, Xoco struck a blow as Manny tried to whirl out of the way, sending his sword flying through the air. Xoco also delivered a kick that sent Manny sprawling on the ground.

The onlookers gave a loud, "Ooooh!" as the favored one went down.

Manny laid there motionless. Xoco rushed forward to him with her blade pointing at his body as she dropped to one knee. Manny quickly turned to face her with the point of his dagger touching the fleshy part of Xoco's chin.

"Do you relent?" Manny said as he breathed heavy.

"No. Do you?" She said with a twinkle in her eyes.

They both smiled and then they both collapsed on the ground side by side. The onlookers cheered for the entertainment they had just witnessed. After a few minutes went by, they stood up, brushed themselves off and returned to where Melanna was standing.

"Amazing! Manny, I didn't know that you had it in you." Melanna said as she poked Manny in the stomach with her elbow. He bent over as though she had lethally wounded him.

"Those pointy elbows will bring any man down," he said as he joked with her.

"Really, you both were very impressive. I can only hope to be half as good as either of you at this," Melanna said as she nodded for emphasis.

"Thanks! It was fun!" Xoco responded then turned her attention to Manny.

"So was it a draw or did one of us win? Which is it?"

"Let's just say we both won and we can both collect our winnings."

Manny gave Xoco a sheepish grin. Xoco decided to play along.

"Okay, I'll go first. Have a seat right here for your hair cut."

She patted a crate that was under the shade trees. Manny complied but secretly wished that she wouldn't butcher his hair. Xoco pulled out yet another dagger from a sheath that she wore around her waist. This one was razor sharp unlike the one she had just sparred with. She planted her feet in front of Manny as she took the ever-present lock of hair that hid his eye and quickly cut half of it off. Manny was sitting with his hands on his knees, palms up. Xoco placed the lock of hair in one of his hands and proceeded to cut more off. Manny started to get up, but Xoco pushed him back down. When she was finished, Manny looked more mature and handsome with a shorter cut. The two young women stood with their hands on their hips and looked him over.

"Okay, you got what you wanted. It's time for me to get what I won."

Manny stood up, walked over to Xoco and placed his finger under her chin to tilt her face up to him. He looked into her eyes as his lips gave her a soft kiss. His lips became greedier as his hands cupped her face. All of the sudden, he felt a sharp prick in his side. He looked down to find her dagger was warning him to stop.

"Hey, you put a hole in my shirt!"

Xoco stepped back saying, "Sorry. Reflexes I guess."

Manny shot her a disbelieving look, but she didn't care. Melanna giggled, embarrassed for Manny.

"Thanks for a good time! And again, it was nice meeting you, Melanna. We have to do this again soon."

Xoco packed her things up and left the training field. Manny managed to introduce Melanna to others who were there to train. It lightened the hearts of those present to see the person that they believed to be the one that was prophesied about.

Amoxtli approached them saying, "Come now. Not a moment to waste. Let's continue with our training, Melanna." He picked up the silver and blue shield and sword that he brought from the temple. "I want you to practice with these a bit and get the feel of them."

She took them from Amoxtli and was immediately surprised how much lighter the sword was as well as the shield.

"Okay let's begin!"

As soon as he barked the order, a man came charging up to her and began to strike at her. She instantly held the shield up in defense. The attacker stepped back two paces in time for

Melanna to extend the point of the sword in his direction. A burst of lightening went from the blade to the attacker and knocked him out cold.

"Oh, my gosh! What was that?" Melanna said as she trembled with shock and fear.

"Not to worry. That is what I wanted to see. You are indeed the true wielder of this sword, for no man could have delivered that power other than the chosen one."

"Is he alright?" she asked, concerned for the man's wellbeing.

Amoxtli went over to check the man's vital signs. A moan escaped the man's lips.

"He'll come around in a minute. Not to worry." Amoxtli stepped over the fallen man to address the group. "Is there another volunteer?"

The large gatekeeper stepped forward that had ushered Manny and Melanna into the training field. He was one of the biggest men there. He also had his doubts about Melanna and her rightful place among the resistance.

"I think that was just luck on your part, princess. Why don't you let a real man show you how it's done," he sneered.

Melanna swallowed a lump in her throat and raised her sword and shield. The man growled loudly and swiftly approached her in attack mode. Melanna whirled to avoid the strike.

"No tricks now. Fight like a warrior! Come to papa!"

He charged again. The magical shield absorbed the brunt of his strikes with ease, one after another. He looked astonished. Steel clashed with steel as the swords came together and locked there for a brief moment. The big man writhed in pain as Power flowed through him. Melanna drew back and then pointed her weapon at the cocky man. A burst of lightening sent him flying backwards. He lay unconscious and sprawled belly up on the ground.

"I guess you won't be telling this tale to your friends around the pub!" Melanna said to her unhearing challenger.

Those within earshot chortled with delight and doubled over in their fit of laughter.

Amoxtli took her aside to say, "I'm very pleased at your use of these weapons. I'll eventually suit you up with the helmet and breastplate that I showed you. For now, I'd like you to continue fencing to give you good fighting skills. Come back every morning to this same place to practice. Can you do that?"

"Yes. If I have to, I'll make up some story to my friends and family. I think that I can pull this off."

"Good! Then I'll see you tomorrow."

Melanna took Amoxtli's hand to give it a quick shake and thanked him for the help that he offered her. She left full of confidence and something she couldn't quite put into words. Could she dare say it was hope? Could it be true that this was her destiny? She welcomed it with her whole heart.

14. THE ENEMY WITHIN

Manny and Melanna left the field and made their way back through the city.

"Wow, you did very good today for your first time. What did I tell you? You're a natural at this."

Melanna acted modest about his compliment but felt good about the praise.

"It *was* fun, wasn't it? But I have to keep in mind that this is a very serious matter. I hope that what we're doing will make a big difference."

"I think so. A lot of other people do too. Just listen to the still small voice inside of you. The Great Spirit will show you all things in his time. You'll see." They stood under a tree as they gave each other a parting hug.

"Later, Mel."

"Bye, Manny. See you later."

Manny and Melanna parted ways as she took to a narrow back street to go back to the palace. As she approached a dark alley, a hooded figure grabbed her and held his hand over her mouth to stifle her scream.

"Who is here to protect you now, princess? I don't seem to see anybody," the attacker whispered in her ear.

The point of a blade pricked her throat as he continued talking.

"Who do you think you are to be favored above your sister when she should be next in line for the throne? She deserves a royal marriage, the praise and the honor, *not you!*"

He twisted the knife to make his point. She made a muffled scream and struggled in his embrace at the discomfort.

"You are nothing more than a pile of rubbish beneath her feet. I should do her a favor by ending your miserable life right here and now, you-"

Melanna bit his hand so hard that he let go. She turned to see the face of her attacker, which was none other than Mulac.

"You! How could you? You're my father's trusted guard! Did my sister put you up to this?"

He swiftly grabbed a handful of her hair and yanked her head back.

"What if she did? Can you blame her? She loves me, you know. But she's also my meal ticket right now, got it? You should just be worried about what I'm about to do to you."

Melanna let out a scream of pain as he jerked her hair harder for emphasis. Something rose inside of her as she twisted out of his grasp and raked her nails across his face. The scratches on his face only made him pause for a short moment and enraged him even more. Melanna's training paid off as she dropped to a crouch and made a circular sweep with her leg, which knocked Mulac's legs from under him. As soon as he was down, she straddled his torso and started pummeling his face with punches. Mulac was caught off guard momentarily. Her punches were easily blocked. He managed to grab her wrists and fling her off of himself. Melanna rolled once and got into crouch mode again. She grabbed a gnarled stick to defend herself with.

Where did this girl learn to fight?

Mulac lunged at her with his dagger. Melanna whirled completely around to avoid the blade while targeting his head with the gnarled stick. Her momentum didn't stop. She continued to beat the air on every side of him, spinning the stick like a baton behind her back and to the front. She dropped to a very low crouch and struck him in the legs, again sending him on the ground. Melanna jabbed the stick into his stomach, which caused him reflexively to sit up in pain. She struck him in the side of his head. He was momentarily stunned as he lay still on the ground. Melanna turned her back on her attacker to look about her. She took a deep breath to settle herself. All of the sudden Mulac grabbed her from behind causing Melanna to give a blood-curdling scream. He sliced her neck from her ear to her windpipe. He meant to cut her from ear to ear, but he was stopped short when a sudden rush of wind followed by a cold hard fist knocked Mulac on his back several feet away from Melanna. Tez was suddenly standing over Melanna with trembling lips as he saw his beloved on the ground. His eyes filled with rage and bloodlust as he charged at Mulac who had scrambled to his feet. Tez grabbed Mulac and body slammed him several times into the stone building before taking Mulac's head in his hands and snapped his neck, killing him swiftly. And then he was at Melanna's side. Blood was streaming down the front of her and eventually on Tez as he held her close. He tore open his wrist and fed her his blood to begin the healing process. She was conscious enough that she drank from him. He picked her up in his arms and carried her the rest of the way home. When they arrived near the palace, Tez carried her around to the back gardens to lay her on a stone bench that was close by her bedroom window. He cradled her head in his lap as he caressed her face and smoothed her hair away with his hand.

After a little while she opened her eyes and smiled a faint smile. He bent down to place a soft kiss on her lips.

"I'm glad to see you finally wake up. We can't have you sleeping the day away like some lazy loafer."

"What happened? The last I remember was that Mulac was hurting me with his knife. And then here I am with you."

"Oh, you won't have to worry about Mulac ever again. I'd say right now he's thinking that it's the hottest day that he has ever experienced."

"What is it that you're trying to say?"

"I'm saying that I put an end to his life. He won't be hurting you or anyone else again. I'm pretty sure he was the one that tried to kill you in the jungle. I should've made him suffer more before I killed him."

Melanna placed her hand on his cheek to quiet the rage in him.

"You know, before he hurt me, he said in so many words that my sister had put him up to it. My own sister!"

She grimaced and closed her eyes. The thought caused more pain than Mulac's knife had caused.

"It's all over for now. Just rest a bit."

A tear trickled down Melanna's cheek and Tez brushed it away with his finger. She was hurt more inside than anything Mulac could have done to her.

"You need to change your clothes right away. I don't want anyone to see the blood on your shirt. You need to keep this a secret."

He took his own shirt off so that she could put it on over her clothes and enter the palace without arousing the curiosity of anyone. Melanna sat up on the stone bench and looked at his bronze body as he handed her the shirt. She sat momentarily mesmerized by his perfection.

Tez held her arms and kissed her forehead as he said, "There is some business that I have to attend to. I'll see you later."

She took his hand to squeeze it and then had to let him go. He disappeared into the plush gardens and eventually into the thick jungle.

* * * * *

Later in the afternoon the king's gardeners were busy trimming the back garden on the palace grounds. It was the perfect time of the day since it provided cooler temperatures. The garden was filled with every kind of palm tree found in that region. Purple orchid trees and white plumeria trees made the air heavy with their fragrant blooms. The climbing passion fruit vines with large blooms attracted butterflies and bees into the garden. They indiscriminately colored the gardens in blue, purple, berry and white. A mango tree, Melanna's favorite fruit, grew in the midst of all the color. It was here at the base of the tree that an old gardener was pulling some weeds and tending to the tree. He hacked away at the weeds with his machete and stopped to wipe the sweat from his brow. He paused to listen to a subtle thumping of something farther back in the garden. He walked several yards and paused to listen again. There it was again. The old man walked a little farther and parted some palm fronds to find Mulac's body swinging from a tree at the edge of the garden. Some large vultures had already been pecking at his head. They flew away in fright after the old gardener appeared. The old man called the rest of the grounds keepers and they pulled Mulac's body down from the tree. They carried the body into the palace to report it to the king. Tetaneeka was lounging in comfort with his daughter Eleuia in the Great Room which was filled with sophisticated furnishings and books. The sun's rays filled the room with a glow while both of them indulged in reading. The men burst through the door unannounced bearing Mulac's body. With eyes wide with shock, Eleuia took a sharp intake of breath as she covered her mouth. She scrambled to her feet and came to stand next to her father. The king came over to inspect the body. It appeared that half of Mulac's skull was crushed in, bloody and matted. The king pulled Mulac's shirt down in order to read what was written in blood on the shirt.

DEATH TO THOSE WHO BRING HARM TO THE ROYAL FAMILY

Tetaneeka let go of the shirt and took a step back.

"And where did you find him?" he asked the grounds keepers.

"We found him hanging from a tree near the back gardens, your majesty," the oldest one answered him.

"Tell no one what you've seen here today. You are sworn to secrecy. We'll have a secret burial for Mulac," said the king as he waved them away.

"Yes, my lord," the men said as they bowed to the king and carried the body below to the lower levels of the palace to prepare for burial.

The king had his reasons for secrecy. He didn't know if Mulac acted alone. And as things were, he couldn't trust anyone, apparently even in his own palace much less anyone outside of it.

Eleuia stood there dumbfounded, not really giving much thought to her lost lover. Her thoughts were only for herself.

What happened that Mulac's attempt on my sister's life ended so badly? I am left to fight my own battles for my rightful place in the kingdom.

* * * * *

Later on after dark, Tez sat in the trees at the edge of the jungle as he watched for movement through Melanna's window. He waited for her to enter her bedroom to lounge before bedtime like she always did before sleep overtook her. When he was certain that she was there alone, he climbed the tall tree that grew at the base of her window and entered her bedroom without a sound. She sat combing her hair in a knee length nightgown. He cleared his throat to make known his presence. She jumped slightly then squealed with delight as she ran into his arms.

"I have so much to talk to you about. I wish that you wouldn't stay away so long. I really need you right now," She didn't really know where to begin.

"Well, I heard that you finally met Amoxtli. He was very happy to meet you. You don't know how proud I am of you and your choice to take your place among the people. I believe in you, Melanna. I am certain that you will do great things from here on."

"Thanks. That means so much to me. I also met Xoco and a lot of the resistance today in the training field. It was an awesome experience. Too bad you missed it."

"Who says that I missed it?" he said with a devilish smile. For in fact, Tez had witnessed the whole session that morning from his vantage point in the trees at the edge of the jungle. He was pretty amused when he saw Melanna have the upper hand with some of the men that would've otherwise scared any other female to death. He laughed so hard at the time that he was surprised no one had discovered him eavesdropping. He only regretted that he hadn't followed Melanna more closely when she was returning to the palace.

Melanna pretended to fool with the hem of her nightgown.

"Did you also know that my father promised my hand in marriage to Lord Chak?" She looked into his eyes for a response.

His warm eyes drank her in as he said, "Yes, I know about that too. And I know how upset it made you. But I assure you that it will *never* happen." He said the words slowly for emphasis.

"How can you say that since he is Zafrina's closest ally? This is all in their plans to keep control of the kingdom and squelch the protests of the people. But now I know that they really mean to destroy the kingdom that my father helped to build. They want to decimate us. They have to be stopped."

"And they *will* be stopped." He came to sit beside her and grabbed her upper arms as he continued to speak, "But the timing has to be just right. You have to be patient and trust me. I'm working with Amoxtli and the best men of the resistance to plan an attack. Can you continue to train and meet with the resistance in secret? Can you do that for me?"

Melanna closed her eyes, trying to agree with what he asked of her.

"Yes, I will trust you and do as you ask. It won't be easy. I loathe that man! He makes my skin crawl."

A strong breeze blew into the window and caused the flame of her lamp to go out. She instinctively drew closer to Tez in the dark. He gave a throaty laugh but held her to him. Her blood, her very essence smelled so sweet to him. Her skin felt warm in contrast to his cooler touch. If she only knew what a real beast that he was or could be, she wouldn't take comfort in his arms. But rather, she would flee in the opposite direction.

"How is it that I'm so deserving of you?" he whispered in her ear as he gently nuzzled her.

"I feel that I'm the one that should be asking that question. You are truly a gift to me."

Her hand slipped under his shirt to caress his chest. She could hear his faint, steady heart beat. Her heart beat much faster and harder and it was music to his ears. He lowered his head to sprinkle kisses on the side of her face and down her neck. He nuzzled her chest below her collarbone and did swirling motions with his tongue, tasting her. She arched her head back in pleasure and moaned. He brought her head up and kissed her long and passionately as if to brand her as his. She melted in his arms. The passion in him grew along with the thirst as his fangs extended. She was like a beautiful fragrant fruit, ripe for the picking. Just one little taste from that delectable neck being offered to him. His eyes grew fiendishly dark as his thirst threatened to take over. What was he thinking?

As his hands held her face on each side and their foreheads touched he spoke in a ragged tone.

"I need to leave before I lose control and decide to devour you myself."

"I'm not stopping you."

She seemed pleased that she could have an effect on him, but she was truly being naïve about the bloodlust of a vampire. Sexual cravings were also much stronger in them than in humans too.

"That's exactly why I have to go."

He smiled in the dark at her. She exhaled deeply and held his hand until he stood to leave out the window that he had entered.

"Will we ever be able to be together and leave all of this behind us?" she asked.

"Yes, my love. I promise you that we will. Be patient. Things will work out."

And then he was gone into the darkness of the night. But his touch and his kisses still lingered with Melanna. She slept a peaceful sleep and dreamed that she was with the man that she loved.

15. HOW DO I HATE THEE? LET ME COUNT THE WAYS

A time to rend and a time to sew, a time to keep silence and a time to speak. Eccl. 3:8

Melanna woke up refreshed the next morning. She got dressed and went down to have breakfast where she found Eleuia seated at a table already eating. Eleuia gave her sister a sneer as she entered.

"You're in a good mood this morning," Melanna said sarcastically. "Would it have anything to do with your boyfriend being found dead yesterday?"

Eleuia whipped her head around sending her hair cascading around her shoulders.

"You don't beat around the bush, do you? And how would you know anything about Mulac and me? Were you eavesdropping or something?"

"No, I try to avoid such things if I can. It helps to keep my food down."

"Ya, go ahead. Laugh it up. But if I hear that you had anything to do with Mulac's death or know anything about it, I'll make you regret the day you were born!"

"You've already tried to make me regret it hundreds of times. I'm tired of it. I won't take it anymore. And don't worry. Soon I'll be leaving the palace for married life. You'll finally be rid of me. You can find someone else to verbally abuse."

Saying this only fuelled Eleuia's emotions more.

"And that's another thing. By the gods, why should you be picked to wed when I am next in line to rule since I am the first born of the king?"

Melanna placed her hands on the table so that her face was closer to her sister's.

"Good question! Why don't you go to Lord Chak and ask him yourself? I don't want to marry him! If you could trade places with me, I'd gladly agree to it! He seems like the best thing that you've ever had anyway. Really! Why don't you pay him a visit?"

"You can't be serious that you don't covet the status that comes with that marriage! And to be wed to such a perfectly gorgeous guy! Are you out of your mind to want to pass that up? What's wrong with you?"

"I don't love him! Why is that so hard to understand? I love someone else."

"Who? Tezcatli? What can he offer you that Chak can't?"

"I wouldn't care if Tez were dirt poor. I love him and he loves me and cares deeply for me. I could never love Chak. I abhor the thought of being joined with him."

This new knowledge gave Eleuia pleasure in knowing her sister's feelings for Chak and being forced to marry him anyway. Death would be too swift and kind to her. Living in a hell seemed better punishment for her.

"Well, sister, too bad you don't know a good thing when you see one. All I want is your happiness," she said sarcastically with her head tilted at an angle as she got up to leave.

Melanna knew that she didn't sincerely mean what she said. It just irritated her. But she was glad that she could eat her breakfast in peace.

She went off to her training and did so for days without raising suspicion. Her fighting skills became quite good; although, she never thought she would be as good as Xoco. Whenever she would go home with scratches on her face or arms, she would tell her father that she was rough housing with her friends again. The king or Qaileen seemed to accept that if it were brought up.

Fight training was going so well for Melanna, that the boys were taking bets to see who could be the one to bring her down. She never passed up a challenge. The boys would taunt her, calling her the "little princess" and "shouldn't you be shopping instead of fighting?" She would always keep her cool and let them have it!

Xoco showed her a few good moves, which she put into good use. A woman doesn't always need a sword. A swift knee to the groin will bring a man down too followed by a strike to the head with the hilt of the sword to finish him off. And of course there are times when a man thinks he has the upper hand when he gets a woman in an ironclad bear hug. Xoco taught her to throw her arms, palms down while at the same time her hips pushed away to free herself. Then retrieve her sword and continue the fight.

A couple of boys could be seen on the ground holding their heads and their crotches in pain after having fought with Melanna. She smiled with certain satisfaction. These were just humans though. Soon she would have to face an army of vampires. Amoxtli realized this fact. He came up with the idea that he should invite Tez to a training session. Melanna was pleasantly surprised to see him there, but she wondered what was really going on. She spent several hours with her regular sword and dagger. Amoxtli walked over to her with the helmet, sword and shield from the temple. He motioned Tez over to them.

"Tez, I would like you to train exclusively with Melanna for the rest of this session. She needs to know what it's like to fight one of your kind."

Tez looked at Melanna and wondered if she was ready for this. She knew what he was thinking.

"Don't look at me like that!" she said. "I need to do this. I'll do it with or without you, so what's it going to be?"

"Okay. But I'll take it easy on you at first."

"Fine! But I won't take it easy on *you*!"

She turned as if to walk further out on the field but she quickly whirled around with her sword as she yelled, "Heads up!"

The swift beat of her heart and the heightened musky wildflower smell that was uniquely Melanna gave her away to Tez. He was ready for her. But he was not prepared for the Power that the sword could deliver. His sword deflected off of hers, sending a jolt through his arm. He did a quick back flip to move out of her path. She advanced on him again. Tez moved with lightening speed to her back. He patted her butt with his sword. She turned with a gasp realizing that in a real fight, she wouldn't have been so fortunate. They paused for a brief moment for Tez to give instruction.

"As you can see, you can't trust your sight when you're fighting a vampire. Lesson number one: once you've engaged in a fight with a vampire, your sword needs to be in constant motion. You need to keep it whirling above your head or allow your body to be in motion, whirling about completely, from the right and also from the left. If you do this, it's as if you envelop yourself with the Power of the sword. Do you understand?"

"I think so. Constant motion or I die."

"Let's hope it doesn't come to that. Again!"

Melanna lunged with her sword and then twirled completely around to defend against Tez. Then she twirled the opposite direction. She combined some whirling motions with her sword above her head and then around her body. Next she proceeded to twirl completely around again, always moving. All the while, Tez swiftly moved about her to try to find an opening. He moved with fantastic speed and his sword clashed with hers when her turns came to a stop. But once again, in between her revolutions, he came up behind her with great speed and placed his sword under her chin. She threw his sword off with her own, rolled on the ground and picked up her shield as she stood on her feet.

Tez gave an approving smile as he said, "Nice!"

Melanna didn't slow down one bit. She crouched low to the ground, sliced through the air at his legs, and continued to whirl around on her way up. Tez delivered some blows to her, but her shield absorbed his strikes as she advanced with her sword at the same time. Tez was not quite quick enough as her sword found its mark on his left side. Tez writhed in pain as the Power of her sword went through him. All of a sudden he wasn't there. The force had sent him plummeting through the air. He was on the ground face down. Melanna dropped her sword and shield and ran to him.

The boys who were watching from the sideline had taken bets for this fight. They all moaned in disappointment and shook their heads at having lost their money.

Melanna dropped to her knees as she tried to roll Tez over. Once he was on his back, his eyes flew open and he grabbed her arms to bring her close to his face.

"Lesson number two: when you've downed a vampire, finish him off. You must either stab him through the heart or cut off his head."

"You're kidding, right?"

He gave her a stern look.

"No, I guess not."

He released his hold on her and got to his feet. Because he was immortal, his body recovered quickly from the wounds caused by the sword. Melanna was impressed by his endurance. Once again he stood before her ready to duel, looking as perfect as he did before the sword fighting, and not a hair out of place. She took a moment to swoon at him.

She moistened her lips with her tongue as she stood there daydreaming.

Just watching Tez takes all the work out of this training. And I thought I wouldn't enjoy-

"Keep your mind on the work at hand please," he said with more seriousness than playfulness.

She wrinkled her nose and her lips pouted. Tez advanced on Melanna as she continued to try to remain in motion to defend herself. When Tez's sword clashed with hers, it was very brief or he would've ended up on the ground again. Sparks flew in the air as well as in their hearts for each other. Their sword fighting began to take on the characteristics of a dance. The movements became flawless and graceful. Fire and ice, strength and passion. Melanna twirled her sword above her and from side to side, turning in circles, stabbing the air, and repeating her movements. Tez with his speed and grace was like a matador waiting for his chance to strike, but ever watchful of the sword she wielded. He finally found his moment to disarm her with a sudden strike of his sword, sending her weapon flying several feet away from her. He embraced her from behind.

"Lesson number three: expect the unexpected," he said as he nuzzled the side of her face.

She closed her eyes in ecstasy at having been conquered by her lover. She relished the feel of his strong arms and his breath on her face.

"Do you yield?" he said with a faint smile on his lips.

Melanna threw her arms palms down, jutted her hips out, and twirled out of his grasp to retrieve her sword. She stood crouching in a sword-fighting stance ready to go again. It was now Tez who stood there admiring her.

They continued to train for a couple of more hours. It boosted the morale of their fellow kinsmen who were training and stopped to watch as they rested in between their own fencing. The two decided to call it quits for the day. Tez walked Melanna half of the way home. They parted ways when they came to the park. Eleuia happened to be with friends on the opposite side of the street as she watched her sister and Tez say their goodbyes. Eleuia noticed that Melanna looked like she had been doing something very physical by the way she was dressed and by the sweat that covered her flushed face and arms. She avoided questioning her sister about her activities. The next morning she decided to follow her. Sure enough, Melanna was dressed in plain clothes again and headed out early. Eleuia was hot on her heels. She stayed far enough away not to be seen and raise suspicion. Melanna entered the training field through the large door. Eleuia decided to circle around through the jungle to gain a vantage point without alerting anyone. She scanned the training field with her dark honey colored eyes and was able to see into the clearing at all the people who were sword fighting. The soft breeze carried the conversation of a few people who were standing on the side and allowed her to hear what was going on. She quickly learned that this was the training camp of the resistance. She stood there twirling a strand of her chestnut brown hair when she spied her sister sword fighting with a bearded middle-aged man. Eleuia stood frozen.

Is he letting her win or is she really that good? she wondered to herself.

Although Eleuia was impressed with Melanna's fighting skills, she seethed inside at the position that her sister was taking.

Melanna is putting us all at risk with this behavior. Father would have a cow if he knew what she was up to.

How could she ruin things for them? And how about her betrothed? Surely this wouldn't go well with him. She watched as the middle-aged man was disarmed and on the ground only to be helped back up to his feet by Melanna to fight again.

Then a plan formed in Eleuia's mind. She would pay a visit to Lord Chak and tell him about the activities of his bride to be. Maybe Chak would change his mind and want to marry Eleuia, the rightful heir to the throne. A smile crept on her face. Maybe the winds of good fortune were blowing in her direction after all. As for the fate of her sister, she could only hope for the worst.

Eleuia waited until the late afternoon to set her plan into motion. She put on her most enticing garment that she owned, one that showed plenty of cleavage and left little to the imagination. She made sure her makeup and hair were perfect. Taking one last look at herself in her mirror, she thought that no one could refuse her. She walked out of her room with confidence. She left the palace and walked through the streets of Coba until she came to the pyramid.

A hooded figure was lighting the torches on the outside of the pyramid. There were guards at the entrance, each holding a spear. When she approached they barred her way into the pyramid. She told the guards that she wanted an audience with Lord Chak. The guard on the left disappeared into the pyramid only to return to guide Eleuia to the chamber where she would meet with Chak. Once she was in the designated chamber, she felt more at ease. She took the liberty of walking around the room and touching odd relics that Chak had collected. There was an obscene sculpture in the room of a nude man and woman that would have made any normal person blush. It only intrigued Eleuia. As she continued to be mesmerized by the contents of the room, Chak silently crept into the room and was watching her.

"Do you like it?" Chak inquired of her while looking amused.

Eleuia flinched at his sudden appearance and tried to catch her breath.

"Yes, I do. It's a fine piece."

"I'm glad that you like it. What can I do for you?"

"I can appreciate what you and Zafrina are doing for the City of Coba. And I admire your plans to want to unite the people of our kingdom. There, however, is a problem that exists that I think you should be made aware of."

Chak came closer and leaned on the wall with his arms crossed over his bare chest as he eyed her with his snake-like stare.

"Go on. I'm listening."

"Your betrothed, my sister, has joined the resistance. I observed her fight training just this morning."

She paused as Chak suddenly perked up at this bit of news and shifted his weight.

"She doesn't even want to marry you. She told me this much herself. I, on the other hand, think that it was a good arrangement. She doesn't realize what a privilege it is to be asked for her hand in marriage by your lordship."

"Do you think that I would fare better if I had asked for your hand in marriage instead?" he asked as he studied her with his unblinking stare. He came even closer.

"Pardon me for saying, Lord Chak, but I am clearly the rightful heir to my father's throne since I am the first born. I have no qualms about marrying someone like you if you were to ask me."

Chak came within inches of her and held her eyes with his as he compelled her to do his bidding.

"You will tell me everything that you know about Melanna. Where is her training camp? Who do you remember seeing there? Who is leading them? We have all night for you to recall the details. But right now, I'm not in a hurry."

He placed his hands on her shoulders and pulled her clothing down to her upper arms while he kissed her shoulders, face and neck. They sat down on a nearby couch while Chak continued his assault. Eleuia lay down on the couch to allow Chak to have his way with her. Her fingers entwined in his hair as he kissed her between her breasts. He made her feel different than any lovers had ever made her feel. It was magic, delicious and dangerous all at the same time. That's why it felt so good. Chak's mouth covered hers in a hungry kiss as he picked Eleuia up in his arms and carried her over to the majestic ivory canopy bed. He could control himself no longer as his hunger caused his eyes to turn monstrously black and his fangs to extend. Eleuia was filled with fear to see his transformation.

Chak once again stared into her eyes and said, "Don't be afraid."

"I won't be afraid," she repeated in a hushed voice as she anticipated his next move. Chak rushed to her throat so fast that she didn't know what was happening. And then she felt the sting and the pressure as he drank her blood. A feeling of euphoria came over her as he drank from her. Likewise, she could feel his pleasure as he fed on her since there was a blood bond made. Chak only took a taste as he planned to prolong this time spent with Eleuia. Her blood dripped down her chest. Chak released her to lap up the dripping blood and to continue to kiss her all over. He sank his teeth into her breast to taste more of her. The pain only lasted for an instant before being replaced by a haze of good feelings. He traveled downward as he bit into her femoral artery of her thigh, but he was careful only to take a taste. He would exact his needs from her both painful and pleasurable. He continued to travel over her body, sinking his teeth in different places, leaving her body bruised and bloodied. At one point, he lay close to her as he began to question her again about her sister's involvement with the resistance and all the details that Eleuia could remember. She shared everything with him that he asked for. Before the sun rose, he got up and walked to the door. When he opened it, some of the subservient vampires were waiting behind the door. They were all very pale but strikingly beautiful, both male and female. They walked into the room and surrounded the bed. Eleuia's eyes fluttered open as she became painfully aware that a dozen eyes were focused on her. Terror gripped her as the group of vampires attacked her in unison. Her screams were silenced quickly. Chak, with a sense of accomplishment, stood there at the door with an evil smile on his face. All in a night's work.

* * * * *

Melanna planned on going to the training camp again as was her usual routine. When she stopped to eat some breakfast before leaving, she was surprised that she didn't see Eleuia anywhere. Even when her sister was out partying, she usually came home, no matter what time of the night it was. At least there would be no confrontation or biting words for her to mull over in her mind this morning. When she was ready, she set out for the training camp. She happened to run into Manny on her way there. He asked if they could chat a while in the park before going over there. She gladly agreed. They sat on a bench near the pond. The birds had all come to life in the early morning light. They displayed high energy with darting in and out of trees and their incessant chirping. Dragonflies flew in wide circles over the pond, landing momentarily on tall grasses at the edge. There was a thin mist in the air that lent to the tranquility of the moment. Manny wanted to save his energy for training so he didn't bother skipping stones on the water. He savored the moment with his best friend. But he seemed a bit nervous. Finally he decided to voice what was on his mind.

"Do you think that Xoco likes me?"

"I don't think that she *doesn't* like you. You're a very likeable person," she said with a faint smile on her face.

"If you don't mind me saying so, I think she is a beautiful woman, a total package. Any man would be lucky to have her."

Melanna noticed that he used the word "man" and thought that indeed, Manny had finally crossed over from boy to man somewhere without her even noticing. She studied his profile and saw a hint of beard on his face. She was too preoccupied with other things to even notice the changes in her friend. Deep down she was proud of the man that he had become and was glad of her friendship with him.

"I totally agree with you that she would make most any man happy."

"I think that I'm going to ask her if she and I can start seeing each other. I think that it will turn out okay as long as she keeps her dagger in its sheath."

Melanna looked amused and they both chuckled in agreement.

Manny changed the subject as he said, "So I heard that they found Mulac's body on the palace grounds near the garden." Melanna nodded her head and wondered if she should share what had happened with her. Should she entrust Manny with Tez's secret? At this stage and taking into consideration what they were up against in the near future, he should know. He was her best and most trusted friend.

"Yes, about that, there is more to it than just that. Remember that day that you, Tez and I went into the jungle to enjoy a picnic?" Manny nodded in answer. "After you left us there, Tez played his flute for me. After he was done playing, he saw a masked man shoot an arrow at me. He ran toward me to protect me and was hit in the back by the arrow. I thought he was dead. I pulled it out of him, but he recovered quickly."

Manny looked unconvinced. "Nobody just recovers quickly from an arrow! And why would someone want to kill you?"

Melanna turned more to face him saying, "That's right. A regular man doesn't recover quickly after being fatally struck with an arrow." She let that sink in. The wheels in Manny's head were turning.

"Are you suggesting that he isn't a regular man?" There was a long pause. "That would mean that you are suggesting that he is immortal."

Melanna tried to shush him and looked around if there were anyone else within hearing in the park.

"That's right, I am. If you think about it, all those weird things that he has done, like when he broke up that entire tree at the picnic site, his speed and his strength, although, you weren't around to witness some of that. Well, it was after I helped pull that arrow out of him that he told me the truth. But he isn't like these other vampires that are trying to destroy our people. He is a victim himself when Zafrina had his wife killed and then changed him into a vampire."

"Wow, he told you all this?"

"Yes, and there's more. You asked why would someone want to kill me? Eleuia had taken Mulac, one of my father's guards, as a lover. She was trying to get him to kill me. At first, it was out of jealousy and bitterness. But then after my father arranged a marriage for me with Chak, that drove her even further over the edge. Mulac followed me after a morning of fight training and nearly killed me in an alley." She paused to show him the scar on her neck that remained from the incident. "He said that it should be Eleuia who was being wedded off and given her rightful place on the throne, not me. If it weren't for Tez, I would be dead. So in my defense, he killed Mulac and helped me make it back home."

"I don't know what to say. I was totally oblivious to all this."

"I'm sure you've had other things on your mind. But I thought it was safe for you to know since he will be fighting alongside us with the resistance. It's important for you to know the truth about things. After all, you are still my best friend."

She laid her head on his shoulder. His hand covered hers which rested on his thigh. They sat there together for a little while longer until they decided not to burn any more daylight. They trekked through the city and came to the dilapidated house at the edge of the woods and knocked on the door. No answer. Manny knocked again even louder. Again, no answer. They made a wide circle through the jungle toward the edge of the training camp. They stood frozen at the edge of the jungle as they stared in horror at the sight before them. Members of the resistance lay dead, their bodies strewn from one end of the field to the other. Men, women and teachers all lay in bloody heaps on the ground. There were no survivors. Manny's first thought was of Xoco, if she were among the dead. He suddenly bolted ahead into the clearing. He frantically looked from one victim to another to try to find her if she was there. He discovered that she wasn't there. Amoxtli was not among the dead either. Manny and Melanna thought it best to head over to the temple and alert Amoxtli or any remaining resistance about what had happened here. They turned to go, but they noticed something strange between them and the door to the outside. Something was elevated on a pole and covered with a bloody sheet that was blowing in the wind.

They approached it, and Manny slowly took the sheet off of the figure. A scream escaped Melanna's lips as they viewed the bloodied and ripped body of her sister Eleuia tied to the pole. Manny knew at once that Eleuia was not a part of the resistance but rather the one who betrayed them. He was only sorry that Melanna had to see this with her own eyes. Melanna bent over crying, full of grief for her sister. Even though their relationship was strained for most of her life, she still loved her. Eleuia didn't deserve to be murdered like this. Manny put a comforting arm around Melanna as they made their way out of the training camp. They walked to the Brotherhood of the Eagle Temple where they hoped they would find Amoxtli safe and inform him of the attack. Manny tried to avoid populated areas as he guided Melanna along. She clung to him in her grief. It seemed like it took them forever to reach it, but it was finally in sight. The ever-present glowing candles greeted them as they entered.

"Hello? Amoxtli? Are you here?" Manny yelled through the temple.

He was worried when at first he got no response. Then a very faint answer could be heard.

"There you are, my friends. I was out doing a bit of gardening behind the temple. What brings you here this morning?"

"We have some terrible news, sir. I'm afraid that the enemy knows about some of the plans of the resistance. They attacked the group that was training this morning behind the old shack," Manny offered since Melanna was so distraught. "And Princess Eleuia was among the dead. She was their calling card to the deed that was done."

Amoxtli immediately tried to comfort Melanna with a hug and pressed her head up to his.

"It obviously is no longer safe to go back there. Next time I want you to follow Tez to our other location that is farther from here."

"You mean, we have more than that location to train at?"

"Yes. That is only a fraction of the people as well as the secret locations where we operate. We don't share that information among the brothers for this very reason if some of us should get caught or killed."

"It's a good thing for the secrecy. If Melanna and I hadn't stopped at the park to talk, we may have been victims ourselves."

"The Great Spirit has chosen you both to be overcomers and lead our people to victory. I'm confident that he is guiding your every step."

"That is encouraging, Amoxtli. But when should we meet with Tez to continue our training?"

"I will send word to him."

His voice trailed off as he and Manny strolled away from Melanna. She stood there in the middle of the temple in her grief at having seen her slain kinsmen. Words utterly escaped her right now. She strolled over to the old artifacts on display. She ran her fingers over the stone relief carving which said, "His spirit soars with the eagles for eternity" and wondered where her sister's soul was right now. She touched the old scrolls and various other objects there. Then she came to the Dagger of Qajawaxal and remembered that Amoxtli said that it deals a deathblow if plunged into the heart of a vampire. She stole a glance in the direction of Manny and Amoxtli. After seeing that no one was watching her, she took the dagger from its holder and hid it under her clothing.

Manny wrapped up his conversation with Amoxtli as they returned to Melanna who was standing by looking innocent yet sad. Melanna slipped her arm around Manny's as they bade the priest farewell. They could only hope to return to their homes without incident after what they had witnessed today.

* * * * *

Zafrina came to Chak's chamber to congratulate him on his dealings with the resistance. He was reclining on his couch with a beautiful human female as he took his time sucking the life's blood from her. She acted as though she were intoxicated, relishing his hunger for her. Her scant clothing barely covered her ample bosom and feminine curves. When Zafrina approached, the female flinched and tried to get up to leave. Chak grabbed her wrist and compelled her to wait there for him. He took a few steps towards Zafrina to speak more privately.

"I understand that you got some inside information about the resistance through Princess Eleuia," Zafrina said amused.

"Yes, indeed, she sought me out to set me straight, insisting that she was next in line for her father's throne. She admitted spying on her sister who is fight training with the resistance."

"Melanna's activities don't surprise me one bit. I knew that she was up to no good, although I never knew that she would go to such lengths. I'm glad that you have things under control though."

"Yes, my queen. Was there something else you wanted to discuss with me?"

"Yes, there is. I think that we should step up the royal wedding before things get too much out of hand. I think that the wedding should be one week from now. Do you think we can pull it off?"

"I'm confident that we could do that. Can you send a message to the bride to be at the palace? She will need to do her final preparations to meet me at the altar."

"I can arrange that," Zafrina said with a smile and a nod.

With Zafrina still standing there, Chak returned to the female on the couch. He took both of her hands and helped her to her feet.

After he kissed her on the mouth he said, "I won't be needing you now. You may leave...by way of the window."

Without hesitation she walked over to the window, stood on the sill with feet together, spread her arms open, and fell to her death on the rocks below. Chak acted like he got some satisfaction at seeing yet another human snuffed out before him. So many humans, so little time.

"Shall we?" he reached his hand out to Zafrina who looked at him with adoring eyes.

"You have such a way with the ladies."

He only looked at her from the corner of his eyes, and smiled with an evil confidence.

As planned, a messenger was sent to the palace to inform Princess Melanna that the wedding was to be held a week from now. Melanna looked aghast when she read the letter. She felt as though she was being smothered by an unknown force. It was hard for her to breath. She ran to her room and flung herself onto the bed as she sobbed into her pillow. Tez happened to be watching her bedroom window from a tree closest to her window and entered her room. He immediately knew that something was wrong as he rushed to her side. She sat up and took comfort in his arms.

"It makes me so sad to see you cry, my love," he whispered in her ear after kissing her forehead.

Melanna managed to pull herself together to speak to him through her tears.

"My sister is dead along with some of the resistance where I trained. And now a message was just delivered from Zafrina saying that the wedding will be held a week from now." She started sobbing again in her despair.

Tez rubbed her back and pressed another kiss on her forehead.

"Take courage, my love. Remember the prophecy. The Great Spirit wouldn't have chosen you if you couldn't be used to overcome our enemies. I'm confident that we are on the winning side. I just need you to go about business as usual tomorrow. I know it will be hard. We can't bring more suspicion on ourselves than there already is. No more training for you. I will meet Manny and take him to the training camp where I frequent. I will fill you in on the details of the fight campaign when we have more definite plans. Can you do that for me?"

She nodded into his chest. He continued rubbing her back and soothing her fears away. A little later Tez started to say goodbye, but Melanna clung to him, begging him to stay with her through the night. He looked into her eyes and melted at the site of her sad expression. He agreed. So they cuddled up in the center of her bed for the night. Melanna refused to give in to hopelessness with her love by her side.

16. GRUDGINGLY MAKING PREPARATIONS

    Melanna had a troubled sleep as the vision of her dead sister tied to the pole at the training ground haunted her throughout the night. At one point when Melanna had drifted off to sleep, she dreamed that she was standing alone at the foot of the pole under a stormy sky. Eleuia's face and body were bruised and bloodied, and she had the appearance of being dead several days. Her eyes flashed open as she stared down at Melanna with a hateful look. Her expression turned to one of mockery and evil amusement as words spewed out like venom.

    "It's because of you that I'm dead now! Daddy's little girl had to run off and play hero, and you didn't even care about the outcome of your choices. Just look at me! It's all your fault, you good for nothing tramp!"

    And then a huge snake slithered out of Eleuia's mouth and started to chase Melanna. She turned to run as the snake struck her calf. Melanna flinched in Tez's arms. Since Tez never slept, he knew that Melanna was having a bad dream. Tears slid down her face. All of the recent events were becoming too much. He brushed her hair back from her face and soothed her fears away. He embraced her and kissed her lips and cheeks. Melanna finally settled back to sleep, unhindered by any more unpleasant dreams.

Eventually, the light of a gray dawn crept through her window. Tez smoothed Melanna's hair as he bade her goodbye in the early morning.

But before he left he said, "It's important that you stay away from gathering with the resistance. It isn't safe. You'll be watched more closely. Stay here with your father until you hear from me or Amoxtli."

She nodded in obedience as Tez kissed her forehead. As soon as Tez was gone, Melanna's mind started spinning in all directions about what she would wear for the dreadful wedding in a week's time. She wondered about how she would rejoin her brethren in the resistance. When would that be? Would Amoxtli bring her fighting gear at the right moment? How could she rid herself of Chak?

Melanna bounced out of bed and quickly dressed. After having breakfast, she went to visit Qaileen to discuss what she should wear for the wedding.

Qaileen spread the clothing out that she had worked on since the day that Chak had asked to wed Melanna. The huipil was a loose fitting cotton blouse that was sewn at the sides with holes for the arms and a square opening for the head. It was embellished with shells, stones and imported colored ribbons. It would be worn with a wrap around skirt. Qaileen would also make an embroidered loincloth decorated with feathers, stones and shells for Chak. Both the bride and bridegroom would wear elaborate sandals. They would also be adorned with feathered masks at the marriage altar. The only good thing about wearing a decorative mask would be that no one would see the disgust on her face at having to stand near a man that she loathed and would soon be bound to.

* * * * *

As soon as Tez left Melanna's window and climbed down the tree, he set out to find Manny. There had to be tighter secrecy now that Zafrina's army was striking out against the resistance. He would take Manny far from the city for his own protection and for more training before things were set into motion. Tez made a quick stop at the temple to inform Amoxtli of his intentions. Then he went into the city and found Manny seated at a table near a vendor, deep in thought and nursing his emotional wounds.

Tez sat across from him and said, "Good morning. Everything okay?"

Manny looked at him with wide eyes, now knowing his secret. His hair still tended to hang over his one eye even though he now had a shorter cut by Xoco.

He blinked slowly and as a matter of fact said, "I know what you are. Melanna told me about you. So are you really on our side as she claims you are? What makes you any different than the other vampires that have overrun this city?"

"Those are fair questions." He nodded and folded his arms across his chest as he went on, "Zafrina ripped my life from me and destroyed my people. She killed the woman I loved whom I had just wed. I hate her with every fiber of my being. I want her gone as much as you do. I didn't ask for this life. But I might as well make the best out of a bad situation."

"Thanks for being honest with me. My only thought is for Melanna's happiness. I care for her deeply. I've known her all of my life. She seems to be walking on the clouds when she is with you."

"I will do my best to protect her. I swear that I will let no harm come to her."

"Thanks. I appreciate the sentiment."

"We need to go now. I will take you to a new location called West Camp where you'll stay until you receive word about what our next move will be. Let's go."

The two of them got up from the table and started the trip to West Camp, another resistance training camp in which the location was even a bigger kept secret. No one took notice of them as they walked with an unhurried pace out of the city and through the jungle. Other people joined them in route, all wearing cuff bracelets with the dancing eagle, signifying the unity of the resistance. They wasted no time with words to console one another over the loss of their brethren. Time was of the essence. Avoiding detection was top priority. By the time they reached West Camp, the sun was about to set. Their bodies and feet were weary. Campfires were being lit and food was being prepared for those taking refuge at the camp. Manny saw Xoco helping to distribute food throughout the camp which consisted of beans, tortillas, and turkey meat. He hurried to her side. He stood there looking really awkward, not knowing how to put his feelings into words.

Finally he flung his arms around her as he said, "I'm so glad to see that you're alive. I was afraid that you had fallen like so many others. I saw the aftermath with my own eyes." He pulled away from her and looked into her face.

"But we have to take courage and have faith in our cause and in the Great Spirit. I'm so glad to see you too. Are you staying for awhile?"

"Yes. I came here with Tez."

"I'm acquainted with Tez. He's a great teacher. You should ask him to show you some fight moves some time."

"I think I will if that is the secret to your fighting skills," he responded with a broad smile. His smile quickly vanished as he asked, "Did you hear about princess Eleuia being killed at the city training site?"

"Yes. Word of that spread quickly. She is suspected of giving information to our enemies. Hopefully she didn't know very much. But I feel sorry for the king and Melanna right now. That's no way for anyone to die, much less royalty."

"I agree. Eleuia has never been my friend, but I wouldn't have wished that kind of death on her. I hope that her soul is at peace."

Xoco nodded in agreement and then continued to serve members who continued to stream into the camp for the night.

* * * * *

Back in Coba, the king's servants went to the lower levels of the palace to prepare Eleuia's body for burial where it was placed after being brought back from the training field. The servants stood there holding their lamps with their mouths gaping open. Except for the presence of the bloody sheet that she had been wrapped in, the spot where she had lain was empty. Upon closer inspection, bloody footprints could be seen starting at the table and going towards the direction of the steps that led out of the palace. The servants looked from the footprints to each other's faces as they quaked where they stood. They frantically made their way to the king to report what they had found. The servants burst into the Great Room where Tetaneeka spent much time reading or entertaining guests.

The king stood to his feet at once saying, "What is the meaning of this intrusion?"

The oldest servant answered, still quaking, "Our deepest apologies, my king, but we have a matter of grave importance, Sire."

"It better not be that my dinner is burned once again! I'll have the head of the cook this time-"

"No, Sire. We went below the palace to prepare Eleuia's body for burial, and, uh, and..."

"Go on! What's the matter with you! Out with it!"

"She is gone, Sire. All that is left are the bloody sheet and footprints leading out of the castle."

"By the gods! Surely, she has not turned into one of those creatures that murdered her," the king said as he stood there with his eyes wide with horror as he stroked his skinny beard. "Night is falling. It is too late to search for her now. We'll resume in the morning."

The servants dispersed as they spread the news about the missing princess. It was a sleepless night for the king as his eyes popped open with fright at every little sound in the castle.

Tez swiftly returned to Coba from West Camp to continue to offer his support to Melanna at this time. As he roamed the palace garden, he caught the frenzied conversation of the servants about the missing body of Eleuia. He climbed the tree and made his way into Melanna's bedroom. Melanna was arranging clothing on the other side of the room. When she turned, her heart jumped in her throat as the unexpected presence of Tez startled her.

"Sorry to startle you, my love. But I felt I needed to warn you about some bad news I just heard."

She crossed the room and they both sat on the bed facing each other.

"The servants have discovered that your sister's body is missing when they tried to prepare her for burial."

"Does that mean that her body has been taken somewhere else and they weren't told about it?"

"No. It was resting below the palace in the sheet that covered her at the training camp. Evidence points that she walked out of the palace."

"Can that be possible?" Melanna said as her brows pinched together and she looked at the floor then back at Tez.

"If she ingested vampire blood before she was killed, yes, it's possible."

Tez could sense Melanna's mounted dread and fear as her heart beat sped up.

"If your sister was dangerous when she was human, she is many times more dangerous now. I will have to stay even closer to you now that she is running around as a vampire."

Melanna looked into Tez's deep dark eyes as her hand caressed the curve of his bronzed beautiful face. His eyes were turning even blacker since he needed to feed. Melanna was just too mouth-watering to be close to when his hunger became strong. He explained to her that he needed to go on a quick hunt and then return to her. She told him to hurry. She would be waiting.

Melanna left one lamp lit. She also pulled the bone dagger from its hiding place and slipped it under her pillow. She climbed into bed and tried to stay awake for Tez when he would return to her. One hour passed, then another. She started to drift off to sleep when she was awakened by a slight creak of the door. She opened her eyes, sat up and scanned the room until her eyes focused on the nude form of Eleuia who was standing near the door. Eleuia had always been an exhibitionist, unable to show any modesty. She was no longer bruised and disheveled. On the contrary, she had an unearthly beauty about her in the moonlight. Her hair was longer, her curves were more feminine, and her skin was opalescent. She moved with more grace and stealth then she did in her human life.

"Did I wake you, sister? I was hoping to surprise you with the new...me," she said as she threw her head back with wicked laughter.

"What do you want from me, Eleuia?"

Melanna's fear grew and was apparent with the rapid beat of her heart and the sweet smell that exuded from her body.

"Come now, is that any way to greet your sister who has come back from the dead?"

She took a few steps into the room where the light from the lamp and the moonlight revealed dried blood around her mouth and chest where she had been feeding on victims.

"I just came here to say that I did a big faux pas in spending the night with your betrothed. Oops." She covered her mouth and laughed in mock embarrassment, but Melanna didn't crack a smile.

"So that's how you came to end up dead. Are you proud of yourself? Not only have you proved what kind of jerk who is arranged to marry me, but once again you've proved what a low life slut you are."

"You know, I'd choose my words carefully if I were you. I'm not the weak human sibling you once had."

"I was tired of your attitude when you were human and I'm quite sure I'm still tired of it now. If anything, what you were in your past life has been magnified as a vampire."

"Yes, it has. Everything that I felt for you, to wish evil upon you or to wish you dead, well, that feeling is *really* magnified right about now." Eleuia paused to sniff the air in the room. "I can smell the scent of another vampire in here. No! Could it be...Tezcatli?" Melanna's facial expression gave her away. "Wait until Zafrina and Chak find out about your boyfriend! I wonder if Chak will fly into a rage knowing that his betrothed is sharing her bed with a vampire."

"It isn't like that! I don't have to justify myself to you anyway." Melanna sat on her knees on top of her bed as she faced her sister. "If I were you, I would make a swift departure before Tez comes back. He won't take kindly to your threats or to you even being here."

"Well, why don't we leave Tezcatli a little surprise when he returns to let him know that he missed out on the fun, shall we?"

Melanna slammed her back against the bed as her hand retrieved the bone dagger from under the pillow. Eleuia came swiftly as a blur to land on top of Melanna with her fangs bared, just inches from her sister's neck. She let out a painful intake of breath as the force of her body impaled her on the bone dagger. Melanna watched in the dim light as her sister's body quickly shriveled up to a mummified corpse. She finally pushed the corpse off as it hit the floor with a thud, leaving the bloodied dagger in her right hand. In shock, she tossed the dagger onto the floor on the opposite side of the bed and laid there with her arms wrapped around herself. Finally, Tez sprang through the window and he took in the site with unbelieving eyes. He shoved the shriveled corpse across the room with his foot and took Melanna in his arms.

"I'm so sorry, my love, for putting you at risk tonight. Please forgive me."

"Well, I have been trained to fight these vampires. If I can't handle one vengeful one, how will I handle a whole army of them?"

"Good point. But I'm sorry that it had to be this way. I'm sure you would've rather remembered your sister differently in her passing."

"Sure I would've. But still there would've been no difference in my memory of her either as a human or as a vampire. She was the same 'ole Eleuia - only much worse. But I'm glad that she can no longer be used by the enemy. She is at peace now."

"What do you think about putting her back where she should be in the first place?"

"Sounds like a plan to me. Need any help?"

"No, I got this." Tez picked up the corpse like a sack of grain over one shoulder and tip toed to the lower level of the palace. He placed the body on the table and covered it with the soiled sheet. He returned to Melanna's room where he stayed for a little over an hour cuddled next to her until she was deep in sleep. He climbed out of her window before dawn. Instead of having the palace cause an uproar over the search for Eleuia's body, Tez cornered a servant and compelled him to go to the lower level of the palace and find the corpse there. The servant ran wildly into the king's bedchamber.

He threw the thick curtains open and exclaimed, "Sire, the body of your daughter has been found!"

The king sat up in bed rubbing his eyes as he said, "This better not be a joke! Have you touched any liquor this morning?"

"No, sire! I just came from beneath the palace. Come see for yourself."

The king threw on his robe and took several guards with him as witnesses as well as protection. The light of the torches filled the dark and musty places of the lower palace as the small mob pressed on. Finally they stood in front of the table. The king pulled back the sheet to reveal the dried up mummified corpse of Eleuia. There were gasps that escaped the lips of some men. She obviously had a transformation of some kind. But at least she had not joined the ranks of Zafrina.

"Tell no one what you have witness here," the king said to his guards.

"Yes, your majesty," they said in unison.

The days that followed were like a haze to Melanna. A religious elder under the guidance of Zafrina was sent to Melanna to provide her instruction about the wedding ceremony. He also gave her a wedding vow to memorize that she would recite to her groom during the ceremony. Her skin got goose flesh as she tried to imagine pledging her love and honor to that monster. Her mind rejected the oncoming doom of the whole affair. She longed for the carefree days that she spent with her friends doing what girls do.

In the meantime, training continued at West Camp. Manny and Xoco spent more time fight training with each other as well as time alone together. Manny's thoughts were about if he were to die tomorrow doing something good, trying to make a difference, at least he had the pleasure of knowing such an extraordinary woman like Xoco. He toyed with the idea of making her his wife and imagined seeing her with their children by a warm fire, telling them stories of how they vanquished the mighty vampires of Coba. And then Manny would come out of his daydream as Xoco would advance on him with her weapons of war. She teased him about having his thoughts elsewhere instead of where they needed to be. Her hair was tied in a ponytail as she trained, but some sweaty strands had escaped and clung to her skin. So she pulled out a cloth to wipe her sweaty face, neck and chest. And then Manny picked up his daydreaming where he left off. This time he imagined that it was his hands wiping away her sweat for her, how he would start at her neck and work his way down her chest. He imagined pulling her clothing away to get the hard to reach places. Manny was jolted out of his daydreaming again when Xoco sneaked up behind him and poured a bowl of water over his head. That did it. He was not about to let that go unanswered. He raced after Xoco who knew that she was in for it once he caught up with her. As luck would have it, they ran in the direction of a nearby creek, dodging other groups of people in training along the way.

Perfect, Manny thought as he saw his opportunity.

When he finally caught up with her, he picked her up, carried her into the creek, and laid her straight in it. She didn't even put up much of a fight. They ended up splashing each other until they both had enough. They both sat in the shallow water side by side to catch their breath.

"Well, at least I'm not sweating anymore!" She said smiling at him.

"No, but it looks like you have another problem," he replied as he stared at her body. Her shirt became semi-transparent as the wet fabric clung to her body. Her skirt was not much better. She gasped in utter embarrassment and crossed her arms over her chest in an attempt to be modest.

He thought quickly and said, "Just stay here. I'll go get a blanket to put around you".

Xoco sat quietly in the creek as she waited patiently for Manny to return. She focused lazily on the rippling current as it made its way passed large rocks in its path. Her eyes caught some movement among the trees on the opposite bank. There appeared to be nothing. But before she looked away, she realized that she was being watched by a patrol of Zafrina's vampires.

She scrambled out of the water and ran with all her might as she screamed, "Resistance, to arms! The enemy is here! Ready yourselves!"

The vampires could've easily overtaken her, but in their confidence of victory, they relished the fight. The resistance immediately made fighting formations. Each warrior was armed and ready to face the enemy. The patrol consisting of eight vampires advanced slowly across the creek and into the open field. Amoxtli, who happened to be visiting the camp, came to stand on some boulders behind his warriors. He held a long staff in his outstretched hand as he closed his eyes and entreated the Great Spirit. The top of his staff had a bone carving of a head of an eagle, which was fixed to a long wooden staff. The patrol continued to walk toward the warriors and came to a stop within 50 feet of them. A vampire wearing a red sash came a few steps forward to speak to the humans.

"Where is your leader that I may address him?"

The warriors looked from one face to the other to see if indeed there was a leader to represent them. Finally Tez stepped forward and addressed the captain of the vampire patrol.

"I will speak for these people. Why are you here?"

"We are here to prevent any illegal gatherings that could be construed as treason against Zafrina, Goddess of the Moon."

"We have every right to be here. And we serve our king, Tetaneeka Achcauhtli. We pledge allegiance to him alone."

"Perhaps you are unaware that Zafrina is the true ruler of Coba and not this Tetaneeka as you have erroneously stated. She is the one that holds the true power as ruler and not that puppet king. She is the one you should be answering to."

"That is a matter of opinion, sir, and one in which we are prepared to defend with our lives if we must."

The leader could sense the Power that flowed from Tez, and realized that he was a vampire.

"You must be Tezcatli. I've heard so much about you. I remember well centuries ago when we came across you and your new bride. Zafrina didn't have need of her, but she had other plans for you." He stood there wickedly smiling at Tez as he displayed his fangs. "It's too bad that you didn't want to embrace the gift that she gave you. Our disagreement is not with you. We battle against these humans to bring them under submission for our queen."

"Well then, your disagreement *is* with me!"

That seemed to be the signal that Amoxtli needed. He slammed the end of his staff on the bolder. A lightning bolt coursed through the clouds to his staff and gathered the energy. The lightening was released in surges of Power that overcame the vampires to temporarily blind them. With a mighty shout, the resistance rushed forward swinging their swords as some of the vampires were immediately decapitated. The rest of the vampires regained their sight in time to engage in combat. There were five of them left.

Tez fought with the vampire captain who was the most skilled of the patrol. Their fighting was so fast and frenzied that the human eye could hardly keep up with what was going on. They fought near a group of trees. While fending off the vampire with his sword in one hand, Tez raised the other one to use his Power over the trees and vines. The unsuspecting vampire was suddenly entangled in vines. The tree branches arched around the captain's body, imprisoning him there. Tez stood in front of him with a sharp ended tree branch in hand. He thrust the branch into the heart of the captain and then cut off his head for good measure. He turned his attention to aid the others against the remaining vampires.

Xoco was on the ground with a male vampire on top of her. The vampire was roaring into her face, dripping saliva and spewing putrid breath. Manny ran over to them and thrust his sword into the back of the vampire. The vampire reared up in pain with an angry loud growl but was not killed. Manny looked bewildered now, standing there with no weapon and unable to help Xoco further. The vampire tried to reach behind himself to pull the sword out. He stood there on his knees as he gave Manny a chilling look. Xoco quickly reached for her sword as it laid inches from her on the ground, and stabbed the vampire in the heart. The monster fell to the side. Manny retrieved his sword, helped Xoco to her feet, and they continued to fight.

A couple of vampires thought that the best strategy would be to take out Amoxtli. They placed themselves on each side of him. Amoxtli became aware that he was being stalked. He once again slammed the end of his staff on the bolder. Power radiated from him in a powerful wave knocking the vampires backwards. Then he continued to whirl around and around like a human tornado as he attacked the vampires with his staff. Amoxtli pulled the bone eagle image from the top of his staff, revealing that it was really a bone dagger hidden inside the staff. He stabbed the unsuspecting vampire to his right in the heart. The vampire quickly turned ashen and hit the ground. The other female vampire stood there stunned as her comrade died at the hand of Amoxtli.

"I'm going to make you suffer for doing that, old man."

"Who's stopping you?"

The female vampire screamed in rage as she rushed forward for the attack. Amoxtli simply pointed his staff at her as a bolt of lightning hit her head, bringing her to a stop. He whirled around, his robes flying out from him, as he plunged the eagle dagger into her heart. She crumbled to the ground as well.

Two vampires continued to fight the resistance. They knew they were outnumbered, so they took humans and used them like shields, threatening to end their lives if they weren't allowed to leave. Tez stood silently behind the unsuspecting vampires as they backed toward him. He drove his hands into the backs of both vampires and ripped their hearts out at the same time. They too fell to the ground. A roar of victory went up from the camp. Their enemies had been slain. The Great Spirit had granted them victory. Similar skirmishes occurred in other resistance camps or on the outskirt of the city. All ended in favor of the resistance, but the absences of missing vampire patrols put Zafrina on high alert.

17. THE BALLCOURT GAMES

Zafrina visited the ruler of Chichen Iza to arrange ball court games for the entire week in celebration of the royal wedding. It was the middle of the week when Chak requested that his betrothed join him to watch the games. Melanna knew it would do no good to say she had a headache. So she reluctantly got ready for the event with the help of Qaileen. Her heart was not in it at all when she readied herself.

When Melanna was ready for the trip, she met up with the party that was traveling to Chichen Iza, which consisted of mostly humans that served under Zafrina and Chak. The vampire entourage traveled separately since they traveled much faster than the humans. They could also feed on unsuspecting small villages along the way. When Melanna's group finally arrived at Chichen Iza, darkness was falling. Torches cast a glow on the massive stone structure of the ball court and the people gathered to watch. Groups of people were assembled on the tops of the walls as well as at both ends of the court. Melanna ascended some steps to join Chak on top of the thick stone wall at the center of the court.

Chak took Melanna's hand and kissed it in greeting as he said, "I'm glad you could join me on this festive occasion." His eyes raked over her body.

She looked away, repulsed by the nearness of him saying, "I've never attended one of these events."

"I'll explain the rules then. The players are given wooden sticks to keep the ball in motion. They are also allowed to strike the ball with their hips and forearms. It is an instant win if a player manages to send the ball through the hoop that is attached to the wall," he said as he pointed across the court. "But if this is not accomplished then the winner of two out of three games becomes the victor."

Just then a group of prisoners who were tied and bound to each other were ushered into an enclosure at one end of the court. Two of the captives were led to center court to play the Mayan ball game. They wore loin clothes, thick girdles, hip pads, and helmets. Melanna looked more closely at the faces of the captive players and realized that they were some of the resistance that Zafrina's soldiers had captured. Melanna was frozen in her fear as her heart pounded, giving her emotions away to Chak. He only looked at her face with his unblinking stare, satisfied that she understood that defying Zafrina would not go unpunished. The referee gathered with the two players in the center of the court. But before the game began, Chak stood to his feet and addressed the referee.

"Halt there, sir. I do believe that the game would be more interesting if they played without the protective gear. Remove them! Now! And let the games begin!"

The spectators sent up a roar of applause. The two players exchanged glances and understood that Chak wanted them to suffer much pain while entertaining the crowd. They obeyed as they looked warily into each other's faces. The two men walked to their places as one man prepared to serve the ball.

The rubber ball that was customarily used for the Mayan ball game was less than nine pounds and smooth. But in this case, sharp rocks had been attached to a nine-pound rubber ball to exact as much pain as possible.

The older man served the ball. His opponent returned it with difficulty with his stick. The older man ran to return it after it bounced off the wall. With much force, the younger swung his stick a little too hard as he sent the heavy ball flying into the face of his opponent, making a huge gash on his cheek. The younger man ran forward to return the ball, which was losing momentum. He sent it sailing into the stomach of the older man, ripping his flesh and bruising him. The man moaned and crumbled to his knees. He managed to pick himself up and go to the starting position for round two.

The younger man served which was returned without much momentum. The ball continued to be in play a little longer. The men tried to use their sticks instead of their bodies as much as possible. The younger man almost put the ball in the ring; the crowd moaned their disappointment.

The older man served for round three. The ball was played back and forth and off the wall as before. The flesh on the players' hips and forearms were bruised and bloodied since they couldn't return the ball with the stick at all times. The momentum became unsteady as the younger man tried saving the ball. He swung his stick a little too hard. The jagged ball flew into the air and struck the older man in the eye socket, instantly ripping his eye out and knocking him out cold. The crowd went wild with excitement and applause. Some of the attending vampires were overcome with blood lust because of the blood that flowed freely from the players. They compelled some human spectators to step into the shadows so that they could quench their fiery thirst.

The old man was dragged away as the victor stood in front of Zafrina, Chak and Melanna. The young man bowed to them. Three men approached the winner. Two of them took his arms and forced him to his knees. The third one stood in front of him and to the side as he swung a sword that decapitated him. His head rolled on the court. Melanna's eyes were wide with shock at what she just witnessed before her. The crowd sent up another loud roar of applause. Tears stung Melanna's eyes as she covered her mouth with her hand. The man with the sword picked the head off the ground and placed it on a rack near a wall of the court that had older skulls on it.

Chak looked at his betrothed and said, "Oh, I failed to tell you that there are no survivors in this game. No winners really, except for the chance to play for Coba's princess and soon to be queen. And of course, traitors of the resistance will not go unpunished."

At the mention of the resistance, Melanna glared at Chak with fear and loathing.

"Please stop this. You've made your point."

"And spoil the fun for all these people? I wouldn't dream of it. You know that I can't do that."

"As a wedding present for me. Please, no more bloodshed tonight."

Chak considered her request for a brief moment. He stood silently looking at her.

"If you want me to continue to go along with your wedding plans, then you will honor my request."

"And if I don't?"

Then Melanna pulled a dagger out and pointed the blade at her breast.

"Then you will have no bride standing next to you at the altar."

Zafrina who was seated on the other side of Chak remained quiet, but she listened to the conversation with a smile on her face.

Chak looked amused as he said, "You're bluffing. You don't have it in you to do such a thing."

"You wanna bet?" Melanna held the knife at her throat and cut into it enough to send a bloody streak down her neck and pool along her collarbone. Both vampires started to salivate after the fresh blood, fangs extending, and eyes darkening. Melanna saw their reaction. It vanished as quickly as it came. Chak was able to remain in control.

"Enough! Put that away. You're making a scene."

"And you aren't with all of the head rolling and gruesomeness of this game?"

He didn't want to push her anymore. He rolled his eyes and motioned for the referee to speak with him. He instructed that the remainder of the games was to be played with the protective gear and a regular rubber ball. There would be no more beheadings. The prisoners were taken back to their cells while the bulkier athletes came out to compete. There were some boos from the crowd, otherwise everyone remained in good spirits.

"Thank you. If you don't mind, I'm feeling very tired from the trip. If you'll excuse me, I think I'll turn in for the evening."

"You do look a little pale." He didn't meet her gaze but instead he stared at the blood on her. "Are you sure you won't stay for the after games celebration?"

Melanna wiped the blood from her with a little piece of cloth that she folded and laid on the seat.

"Yes, quite sure. But thank you for being such a gracious host," She almost bit her tongue with that compliment as she gave a subtle bow.

He nodded to her his acknowledgement, sending her on her way. After she had gone, Chak picked up the piece of cloth with her blood on it and put it to his face, inhaling the scent of her. Zafrina looked disgusted.

"Oh, put it down! It isn't like you've never smelled blood before."

"She has a unique scent, like musky wild flowers, untainted and innocent. When was the last time you had a human like that?" he asked with a smirk on his face and looking at her out of the corner of his eye.

"I have had them all! But I must say that female virgins do tend to taste the best."

"You are just too wicked for your own good." He smiled at her adoringly.

Melanna slipped away down the stairs unnoticed by the spectators. She walked on the pavement through the many "thousand columns" until she came to an open field where there was a great cenote and an old bent tree. She stood at the tree, leaning on it for support as she covered her face with her hands and started to cry. And suddenly Tez was there embracing her. She buried her face in his chest as she sobbed.

"Please don't make me go through with this. I want to escape this nightmare that has become my life."

"I'm here, my love. Please trust me that things will go as planned."

He looked intently into her eyes. She was melting again under his look of love for her. How could she not trust this man? He took her in his arms as his lips claimed hers. His kisses became urgent as he pressed her body to his, as if he wanted to unleash the fury of his need for her. She felt as if there were fireworks going off inside of her. She kissed him back and wove her fingers into his thick dark hair. His breath was sweet on her face. Was she still standing? It felt like she was soaring.

He pulled away with a ragged breath saying, "You have no idea how much I want you right now. You have branded my very soul. I love you with every fiber of my being."

"And I love you too, more than you can know."

He breathed deeply to gain control over his emotions. Melanna clung to him as he stroked her hair.

Tez reassured her saying, "You can get through this. I know you can. Remember who you are. And remember that you won't go through anything that you won't be able to bear because in your weakness, the Great Spirit is strong."

She closed her eyes and nodded in agreement and then looked at him again.

"Do you believe in me? That the prophecy is true? And that I can lead the resistance to victory?"

"Yes, of course I do. I have no doubt. Listen to the voice inside of you. Trust it."

He pressed a kiss to her forehead and smoothed her hair away from her face. They sat in silence under the old bent tree while listening to the roar of the mob at the ball court.

Then Tez said, "It was this very spot that your mother gave birth to you those many years ago. I was right here with her."

Melanna had been reclining against Tez, but she sat up to look into his face. He looked so young and handsome as he relived in his mind that brief moment with queen Almika.

"I saw her toss this into the cenote." He pulled a chunky gold ring from his pocket and handed it to Melanna. She held it in the palm of her hand as she studied it in the low light.

"I knew that one day I would be giving it back to you."

Her eyes were wide with wonder at the thought of her mother wearing the very ring that she now held in her hand. She was also sitting in the very spot that her mother had when she gave birth to her.

"After your mother died, I remember hearing the gossip about this ring. It is suppose to be a very old family heirloom that has been passed down from mother to daughter for many generations. They searched everywhere for this ring. I didn't have the heart to give it up until you were old enough. I'm glad that it wasn't lost among the debris at the bottom of that cenote. At least you have *something* that belonged to your mother. You can feel a connection to her through it."

"Tell me about her please. What do you remember?"

"You are very much like her. And although, we didn't say very much to each other, I could tell that she was a woman of integrity. She was as beautiful inside as she was on the outside. I'm sure that she is smiling down on you right now."

He paused as he leaned against the old tree, taking Melanna in his arms. She reclined against him once more. And they both looked into the starry sky, hoping to catch a glimpse of a sign from heaven that indeed her mother was watching her. All of a sudden, a shooting star streaked across the sky as if right on cue.

"That was her way of saying 'I love you'". He gave Melanna a squeeze.

Melanna tried broaching the subject of the battle with Zafrina's army.

"Do you have any definite plans to share with me on when we attack? Or where my weapons and armor will be?"

"The attack will begin on the morning after the wedding ceremony. Amoxtli will place your armor in your honeymoon suite."

Melanna bolted up, spun around and said, "Wait! You can't be serious that I'm really supposed to marry that monster! Why can't we attack the morning before the wedding day?"

"Because there are too many people working on the wedding plans. The vampires will be on alert. After the wedding, things will be winding down. We'll catch them off guard. We've discussed this with the different captains of each camp and Amoxtli. They are all in agreement. So I'm sorry if you don't agree with our strategy, but it's the best we can come up with."

"You could've at least let me in on your so called strategy."

"The less you know, the safer you are. You're too close to the situation."

"You only left out one important thing. It will be my honeymoon night. Do you really want the marriage to be consummated?" She paused and searched his eyes for an answer, pleading with him with her own eyes.

"Of course not! I'd rather rip his limbs off than to subject you to that."

"Well? Do you have a plan for that?"

"No, and if I did, I don't think I'd tell you. Remember? 'The less you know...'"

"I don't like this one bit! It seems that neither party has my best interest at heart." She stood up and glared down at him. "I won't stand idly by while an evil vampire plans to jump my bones, whether it's in passion or blood lust."

"And I don't expect you too. I have every confidence in you that you'll fight him off. You do very well for a woman. I mean-"

"Tez, that's not what I want to hear!" Melanna was standing there with her arms across her chest and fighting back tears. "If you love me as you have said you do, you wouldn't allow this to happen."

He stood up and tried to grab her arm, but Melanna shook off his grip from her.

"Please, Melanna. You need to stay strong and focused on our real goal here. Do not mistake my lack of cooperation as apathy. You are the dearest, most important person in my life."

"I think I'm done here for the night." She gave him an icy look. "I have to plan how I'll save my own skin since my true love is not stepping up to the plate to do it."

"Can I at least kiss the bride-to-be before she is wed?" he asked, somewhat amused by her temper.

She raised her hand with her palm out as if blocking any attempt at closeness.

"Goodnight, Tez. I'll be a married woman the next time you see me. It will be Mrs. Kojolaxel to you!" she said as she walked away without turning to look at him.

"Not if I can help it!" he replied in a low voice that she couldn't hear.

Later that evening, when the crowds dispersed and the ball court was empty, Tez broke into the prison and set the captive members of the resistance free. He instructed them to go to West Camp, which was still considered a safe haven. He compelled the human guards that they wouldn't remember anything about the escape. He also instructed the guards to sleep until their replacements came. When the same guards were questioned the next morning about the escaped prisoners, they were killed instantly for having failed at their job.

Melanna returned to Coba the next day. The wedding was in two days. She wanted to spend her remaining time with her friends before that dreaded day came. But then she thought to herself that it would be a day of emancipation for the human race. A day to rid themselves of the demons that have overrun her beloved city. It was time to take it back and to live life as it was intended.

18. THE WEDDING DAY

A time to love and a time to hate, a time for war and a time for peace. Eccl. 3:8

Melanna laid in her bed as her mind raced. It was the morning of the dreaded wedding day.

Father, how could you do this to me? Don't you love me at all? Don't I mean anything to you?

Her heart ached because of the deep rejection that she felt. She thought about just running away, but what good would that do? They would just find her and bring her back. If she were to end her own life, there would be no "prophesied one" to fight in the battle. It would be the beginning of the end for her people. And what about Tez? She could not do anything foolish to disappoint or hurt him.

Melanna busied herself with putting some clothes on when Qaileen came into her room with a breakfast fit for a queen. She also carried a small vase with wild orchids in it.

"Wow, Qaileen, you shouldn't have."

"Oh, yes, I should have. This may be the last time that I'll get to serve my little Melanna before she becomes an old married lady."

Melanna wrinkled her nose and giggled. She took the vase and inhaled the heavy scent of the orchids. Then she reached for a bowl of mixed fruit.

"What is father up to?"

"Oh, he's in the Great Room reading. But he is mostly just sitting there thinking. I think he is finally realizing that you will be leaving the palace. He will only have servants living here and tending to his needs."

"That's so sad. I haven't talked to father yet. I've been mad at him ever since he promised me to Chak."

"You know, it would be a good idea for you to have a heart to heart talk with him. It may be the last chance that you have to do it before this is all over. And you should really show him what a brave, responsible woman you are."

"I think that I can eat some humble pie and do that. I want things to be right between us before I leave here."

"Good! I'll see you soon to help you get ready for the wedding."

Melanna wished that she could slow down time right at that moment. She finished the delicious breakfast that Qaileen brought to her. After coaching herself on what she would say to her father, she made her way to the Great Room where she found him sitting at a table starring at a mug of hard liquor. She sat in a chair beside him. Everything that she had planned to say to him was suddenly forgotten. Her eyes stung with tears which she tried to hold back.

"This will be your last chance to speak to me as a single lady," she tried joking. It didn't help his mood much. "Well, you will finally be rid of me so that you can have your wild parties here in the palace and act like a true bachelor."

That got a little response from him.

He smirked and said, "But it won't be the same without you. Without my beautiful daughters. I feel like everything good has been taken from me and I am left with nothing but this empty palace."

Tetaneeka felt like crying at that moment, but he didn't want to show any weakness in front of his daughter.

"Father, someday the sound of tiny feet will run through your palace again. Don't be sad. We'll get through this."

"I'm sorry that I have not always been there for you. To be honest, I've never stopped blaming you for your mother's death. But I know now that life is not always fair, even to a king. For the most part I've had everything a person could possibly desire. But I failed to see that my real wealth was my two daughters living under the same roof of my palace. I should've taken a more active role in your lives. I know it's a little late to be asking this, but will you forgive me? I've been such a fool to have neglected you. And now I've gone and done another foolish thing by promising you to Lord Chak."

He paused for a moment as he shook his head with a hand over his eyes.

"I have a really bad feeling about this guy. I am sorry that I've failed you as a father."

Tears glistened in his eyes with his confession. Melanna was overcome by a whirlwind of emotions. She wrapped her arms around him as the tears came unrestrained down her cheeks. He in turn embraced her and cried the tears that washed away years of bitterness. His tears soaked his beard and the shoulder of his daughter. In that moment, Melanna felt peace in the midst of her storm. All of those years of pain seemed to burn away in this one simple act of love between a father and his daughter.

"Father, I forgive you. And I love you. Don't forget that, no matter what happens from this day on." She placed a kiss on his wet cheek. "We'll get through this. The power of the Great

Spirit is at work in our lives. He won't forsake us if we let Him guide us."

Tetaneeka looked intently into her eyes and simply nodded his agreement.

"I'm proud of you, daughter. And you continue to make me proud. You are more like your mother every day." He placed a kiss on her forehead. "You should go now since you have much to do today. And may the Great Spirit be with you as you have said."

He took her hands and squeezed them as he gave her a brief smile. Melanna felt like a changed woman, lighter than air. What love and reconciliation will do to the heart!

* * * * *

Tez sat in the trees at the edge of the jungle as he watched and waited with anticipation when he could follow Chak as he left the pyramid. As fate would have it, Chak left early in the morning to do some small errands on this his wedding day. A foggy mist filled the air and aided in the cover that Tez needed. He slipped down without a sound and followed Chak as closely as he dared. Once Chak was out of the range of hearing of both vampires and humans, Tez decided to confront him. He ran ahead and nonchalantly leaned on a tree to the left of the path. Upon seeing Chak approach from over a hill, he cleared his throat alerting him to his presence. Chak nodded a greeting.

"I heard that congratulations are in order for your marriage to princess Melanna."

"Thank you," Chak responded as he eyed Tez up and down. "Will you be attending the wedding, sir?"

"Most definitely. I wouldn't miss it for the world," Tez gave a sarcastic smile.

"Might I inquire if you are a friend or family to the bride?"

"You could say I'm a close friend of the bride."

Chak inhaled deeply and realized that Tez didn't smell like a human. On the contrary, he smelled very much like a vampire.

"I wasn't aware that Melanna associated herself with vampires."

"Oh, I'm not just *any* vampire. I've known her for a very long time. And I'm here to see that no harm comes to her."

"Well, you know, that doesn't exactly fit into my plans today."

"I know all about your scheme to kill Melanna and to put an end to the resistance. But I'm here to put an end to you instead." Chak's gaze became stony at hearing these words. "I happen to love her very much. I would give my life for her if needed."

"Something tells me that you may end up doing just that! Why don't you join the winning side instead of wasting your existence with the humans? I would rather fight with you, not against you," Chak said as his eyes roamed over Tez's form.

Tez cringed inwardly at the thought.

"Get use to disappointment. I'm here to see that you never take another victim from this city. You can count on that."

The two vampires started to circle each other, sizing up the other and waiting for the other to strike. Chak made the first move by pushing Tez in the chest with such force that it sent him careening towards a large tree. Tez used the momentum to ricochet off the tree and fly into Chak head first with his hands around Chak's neck. Tez sank his fangs into his neck on impact. Chak pulled him off but not without great effort. Tez somersaulted in the air and landed on his feet in a crouched position, waiting for the next move. Blood streamed from his lips and down his neck. He spit some of the blood from his mouth as if it had a foul taste to it. Chak began picking up large boulders and tree trunks to hurl at Tez. These were easily deflected. Tez raised his arms and summoned the thick green vines that covered the ground to entangle Chak to immobilize him. These were not thick enough to hold him, but it bought Tez some time to grab a sharp branch and plunge it into Chak, missing the heart by inches. Chak let out an angry cry and freed himself from the natural confines. He slashed his long nails across Tez's face. The slash marks healed within seconds but left trails of blood. He backhanded Tez, sending him sailing through the air to land with a thud on his back. Chak summoned a swarm of rats to devour Tez where he laid. The furry creatures came suddenly out of nowhere with red glowing eyes and a hunger for his flesh. Tez jumped to his feet and raised his cuff bracelet towards the sky as he entreated the Great Spirit to aid him in his fight. The cuff bracelet glowed with Power. Suddenly flocks of Harpy eagles, small falcons, owls, and other birds of prey swooped onto the scene to shred the vermin with their talons and sharp beaks.

The two vampires ignored the scene as they ran towards each other, leaping into the air. Their bodies slammed into each other as fists flew and fangs missed their mark. As they fell to the ground to land on their feet, Chak tried his gift of mind control on Tez. He tried to make Tez see the illusion that his hands were cut off. Tez stared down at what he thought were bloody clumps that use to be his hands. Likewise, his feet resembled bloody stumps that were dragging parts of his mangled feet. Chak took advantage of the moment and started to pulverize Tez's head with his fists. He picked Tez up and body slammed him to the ground. He continued to bang Tez's head against the rocky surface of the ground which was now covered with blood. Chak hesitated, standing up to admire his handy work. Tez's bracelet glowed again with Power. Heavy mist covered the ground, helping to conceal Tez from sight. A thick woody briar came out of the ground and wound repeatedly around Chak, imprisoning him. The thorns ripped into his flesh as he struggled. The briar encircled his head several times, threatening to block his view completely. Tez lay on the ground, bloodied and broken, with his hand extended to cause the briar to do his work for him. He found the strength to pull himself to his feet. Tez stumbled towards his attacker with a large pointed branch in hand. His vision was blurry, his feet were wobbly. How could he finish the fight in this weakened condition, in need of blood? He needed to feed to replenish his strength and heal his wounds.

Chak stopped struggling to watch the weakened vampire approach him. Some rats that escaped the predatory birds had climbed up the thorny briar behind Chak to chew away at them on the brink of freeing him from his confines. He smiled in the face of his adversary, thinking that certain victory was near.

"I'm going to finish you off here and now. I can't be late for my own wedding. Melanna is just another frail human in a long line of them to chew up and spit out. Soon the city of Coba will be at my feet."

Chak continued to struggle against the briar to free himself.

What is taking those miserable rats so long? he thought to himself.

The anger rose inside of Tez and boiled to the surface. His eyes became fiendishly dark. His strength returned, his sight became clear, and his mind was filled with one purpose. A loud roar went up from the battle zone causing the tropical birds to fly in all directions as if they were fleeing certain danger. Then all was dead silent.

* * * * *

The air was filled with the sound of a ceremonial gong calling the people of Coba to the royal wedding. It was noon time. The ceremony was being held not far from the park that Melanna loved to visit. There was a large grassy meadow with large shade trees on the perimeter. A marriage canopy was set up under some trees. It was adorned with wild flowers and ribbons.

The people of Coba assembled themselves under the shade trees. Children even climbed the trees to get a good vantage point over the heads of the adults. A small group of musicians played a popular wedding song on the flute, guitar and drums. Young girls in festive colorful dresses pranced down the center of the meadow and spread flower petals as they went before the wedding party. Melanna and her three close friends walked solemnly down the same path towards the wedding canopy where a Mayan shaman and her betrothed were standing. Nelli, Zonya and Teela stood on the left of Melanna with bouquets in hand. They wore bright colored festive dresses, and their hair was braided with ribbons. Melanna wore the wedding clothes that Qaileen made for her and a wedding ceremonial mask. No one could see the sad face of Melanna under her mask as she went through the motions. She carried a grand bouquet of wild orchids. Her bride groom wore the loin cloth that Qaileen made and likewise a ceremonial mask as well. In his right hand he carried a staff that was adorned with feathers and shells. It represented that power was being given to him through the marriage to the princess of Coba. The bride and bride groom knelt before the shaman who started chanting in an ancient language as he placed his hands on their heads. This lasted a few minutes but to Melanna it seemed much longer. Beaded headdresses with feathers were placed on the bride and bridegroom where they knelt. The shaman took the right hand of the bride and the left hand of the bride groom and joined them together, signifying that they were now married.

The people of Coba raised their voices in unison, "All hail, our leaders of Coba!"

Then the shaman took a woven bird cage full of yellow, red and turquoise colored birds and released them back to the wild. This was symbolic of the new life of the newlywed couple. They were forever joined as one. And it also marked the beginning of the wedding celebration.

It was the custom for the newlyweds to go directly to their bridal suite and consummate the marriage. They were not to join in the celebration until this had been completed.

After the couple stood up and faced the citizens of Coba, Melanna took her ceremonial mask off to wave at the people in greeting. She turned to embrace her friends who were standing by with tears and smiles.

The newlywed couple walked at a leisurely pace through the crowd of well wishers who threw handfuls of flower petals at them.

An old renovated Mayan house which had been vacant for nearly one hundred years, its original owners long dead, was only a short distance from the wedding ceremony. The newlyweds crossed the threshold and closed the door to all the masses of people who would now start to party in the streets through the evening and wee hours of the morning.

The couple could now relax and let nature take its course. Melanna laid her beaded headdress on a table along with her bouquet of flowers. Her new husband went to the back of the house for a moment alone, no doubt to pull down the bedding. What was the rush?

Melanna swallowed hard and listened. She had no time to waste. She had to pull her mind from the festivities to concentrate on the impending attack of the resistance. She reached for the bone dagger that was tied to her right thigh and walked slowly but cautiously to the room where Chak was.

When she approached the door, she looked around the corner at the back of his head. What was he holding? It looked like a very large knife that glinted in the dim light.

Melanna charged at him with the dagger held poised to strike him. The man turned swiftly to catch her wrist in defense as they struggled. They fell onto a wool rug piled with huge plush pillows that had once covered the bed. Melanna was on her back, still holding the dagger to his heart. They rolled off of the pillows as they struggled with each other. Melanna tried to crawl away from her attacker, but he grabbed her ankle and started to pull her to himself. She grabbed a heavy bronze vase from a low table and wacked him in the head. The force of the blow made a gong sound. Melanna kicked him in the groin and then pounced on him. He let out a deep moan of pain as one of his hands cradled his head and the other covered his groin to protect himself from further attack.

During this time, a few of the old maids of the city gathered at the front door with their ears against the door to listen to the newlyweds' progress. At hearing some of the commotion, the old ladies looked at each other with devilish glee in their eyes and giggled to each other. They were satisfied that things were going as planned with the young lovers. They turned to leave, anxious to spread the news.

Inside the house, Melanna finally straddled the body under her. She poised with both hands in the air to drive the bone dagger into his heart. The man's free hand slipped the mask from his face. Melanna's mouth fell open in shock as she saw the face of her beloved Tez staring back at her. The dagger fell to the floor. They wrapped their arms around each other and covered one another with passionate kisses.

"Hello, Mrs. Tezcatli Uetzcayotl," he said with a large smile on his face.

"Oh, that sounds so good right about now." Melanna was so happy and relieved that she started crying. "How did you manage to switch places with Chak?"

"I sent him on a permanent vacation, somewhere very hot, I presume. He won't be bothering us anymore."

"Are you alright? Did he hurt you?"

"Yes. But I healed quick enough to join the bride at the altar. I didn't want to miss the honeymoon for anything! And speaking of healing quickly, you have dangerous feet too!"

He placed a soft passion kiss on her lips. She felt her insides melt under his touch. How could she have ever doubted that he would be there for her?

"I'm sorry that I doubted you. Will you forgive me?"

"There's nothing to forgive, my love." He pressed a kiss inside her palm. "We have some time to ourselves before the battle begins. We better enjoy the moment while we have it. We don't know what the true outcome will be. And there isn't anywhere that I'd rather be right now then right here with you, my wife."

Melanna blinked her tears away as she agreed with him in her heart. Time was precious. She was fortunate enough to have this man in her life, already making sacrifices for her before they had even married. What would it be like to spend an eternity with him?

Tez and Melanna ignited with unbridled passion that they felt for each other. It consumed them both. The world and its evils outside melted away. It was only the two of them, feeling the heat of the moment. Clothing was torn and scattered about the room. They were oblivious to the furniture or the walls that were in the way. Finally, somehow they made it to the bed and fell onto it. Nothing stood in their way now of fulfilling the fiery desire to be one. This moment was theirs and they reveled in it. They memorized every curve, every line of each other's body. The pace of their heart beats matched as they shared the gift of love that was given to them this day and as their spirits soared on the wings of passion. They gave of themselves freely all through the night. And sun rays of a new day reminded them of what lay ahead of them. They slowly came down from their cloud of ecstasy and returned to reality. But never had they felt so fulfilled then in that moment. Together they could face anything.

19. THE FIGHT FOR FREEDOM

A time to kill and a time to heal, a time to break down and a time to build up. Eccl. 3:3

Two hearts were on fire, ignited by mutual love and adoration. Tez was finally overcome by the sweet fragrance of Melanna's blood and his growing need for her. In the midst of their love making, Tez gently bit into her jugular vein and drank from her, making a blood bond. There was a spiritual and emotional connection made when he drank from her. Melanna could experience what Tez was feeling, and together their spirits soared higher than either of them had ever gone.

When they lay side by side and Melanna had drifted off to sleep in his arms, Tez did some thinking about the battle yet to come. He was uncertain whether they could achieve complete victory over their enemies. If fate would have it that Melanna's life would end on the battle field, he would rather that her death transform her into a vampire instead of losing her altogether. It was completely selfish of him to feel that way, but he simply couldn't go on living without her. His existence would seem meaningless if that happened. He would rather die, but since it was hard to kill a vampire, that would be a difficult thing to do. So Tez lay there for some time, staring at the ceiling and gently stroking Melanna's sleeping form.

After two hours went by, she woke up and asked, "Hey, you, what are you thinking about?"

He let out a deep breath and replied, "I'm thinking about the possibility of losing you during the battle and spending the rest of my existence without you."

"I wish there was something I could say to chase your fears away, but the truth is that it could happen."

"I'm not ready to accept that. There is another way."

"What are you talking about?"

"If you drink my blood and you die today, you would become a vampire. We could still be together." He gave her a moment to let that sink in. "How do you feel about that? Have you ever thought about it?"

"Not really. I haven't thought beyond ridding this city of Zafrina and her vampires. I have not even considered it. What would really change in my life?"

"The most important change would be your diet. Human food will no longer appeal to you, in fact it will make you sick if you eat it. Except strong liquor which really isn't fit for human consumption. That's why vampires can drink it. You will have a constant craving for blood, especially for the next several months of your new life."

"Okay, you seem to handle yourself well in that department. What other changes are there."

"You're body basically has to die to become a vampire. There is a total transformation that takes place. Your organs will be rearranged because of your new lifestyle. You will still have a heart, but it's much stronger and resilient. Sight, hearing and smell are magnified. Everything becomes stronger and more predatory-like in nature. Also emotions are on a much deeper level than human emotions."

He paused for a moment to caress her face and kiss her mouth.

"Why do I get the feeling that you're leaving something out?"

He sighed and reluctantly went on. "When a person becomes a vampire, he never changes. And because vampires never change, we cannot have children of our own."

"Wow. That never really entered my mind. But now that I think about it, it's very sad. But still, it sounds much better than dying. I quite honestly never really saw myself as a ruler of Coba with my children destined to follow in my father's footsteps."

"I was hopeful that you would turn out to be a good queen after seeing you grow up over the years. But times are changing at a quick pace. We could see an end to your father's reign and the whole Mayan empire as a whole.

Word has traveled about the Spanish "conquistadors" that want to come and conquer these lands. We've been keeping an eye on the situation. They have already attempted to conquer the city of Catoche to the South West of the Yucatan. Fortunately, the natives there defeated the Spanish as they sailed away without even replenishing their diminished water supply. They come here for different reasons, and none of them are good. They are looking for slaves to take back to the island nation of Cuba to work in the mines and agriculture. Some come for gold and others try to convert the natives to another religion."

"Do you think that they will come here to Coba?"

"Absolutely. They seem bent on discovering new worlds for their king. I have also heard word that the diseases that the Spanish bring with them kill more natives than their soldiers do."

The information that Tez was sharing with Melanna seemed overwhelming to hear all at once as she placed one hand over her eyes and shook her head in denial.

"If it isn't evil sadistic vampires, it is man himself that we have to fear for our existence! Yes, sadly the world is changing fast."

She snuggled into his neck for comfort for a brief moment. Then she suddenly came to a conclusion.

"But to answer your question, yes, I would rather spend the rest of my existence with you then to die on the battle field and be lost to you forever."

"Are you sure you wouldn't need more time to think about it? Once it's done, you can't go back to being a human again."

"It's really a no-brainer. I know that I want to be with you. Even if we didn't have these major obstacles in our lives, I will eventually grow old. I don't want to be with you that way. I want you to have me while I'm still young and pretty, with all of my teeth and no grey hair, and not shriveled up like an old prune." She smiled a little smile and closed her eyes, waiting for his answer.

"Then that is your final answer?"

She looked into his dark eyes and nodded yes. Tez's fangs extended as he bit open his arm and gave to Melanna to drink. She didn't hesitate to drink from the arm that he offered her. There was nothing special about the warm fluid that traveled down her throat as far as tasting like normal blood. She did, however, experience some of Tez's memories for the past two hundred years as she drank his blood. They flooded her mind like fast moving images. She relived his memory of his first encounter with Zafrina and when he transformed into a vampire. She also experienced Tez's bloodlust when he killed those men of the brotherhood and the redemptive Power that changed his life. Years of loneliness, of heartache, of bloodlust, and of desperate hope all passed through her mind in a whirlwind of blurry pictures until her birth. The images slowed down. A sense of peace and of purpose could be felt.

Melanna stopped drinking and opened her eyes. Tez took his thumb and wiped the blood from her lips. They kissed tenderly and pressed their foreheads together as they embraced.

Just then a sound could be heard as a note had been shoved under the front door. Tez walked to the entrance to retrieve it. He walked back to Melanna and they both read the words penned by Amoxtli.

> We assemble in one hour and take the pyramid by surprise. Put on the full armor in order to withstand the enemy.
>
> Look into the chest by the bed. And may the Great Spirit be with us all.
>
> ~ Amoxtli

Tez walked over to an old dusty chest and opened it. Sure enough, it contained the matching silver and blue sword, shield, helmet and breastplate from Amoxtli. Melanna knew that she should've eaten something to give her the energy she needed for battle, but there was acid in her throat. She would operate on pure adrenaline for the majority of her day. Their mood had grown somber as they dressed and prepared themselves. They clasped each other's hands, and with forehead to forehead they asked for the blessing of the Great Spirit. They took some gear and weaponry in hand and walked out to the edge of the jungle.

The sun had not risen. But the sky was grey and it was yet eerily silent in the jungle. They joined with others of the brotherhood. Their numbers increased as they got closer to the pyramid. The eye couldn't see where the group ended or began.

Finally as the first rays of sunlight lit the top of the pyramid, the brotherhood gave a thunderous shout, enough to wake the dead. And indeed that is what happened. A large mass grave that was behind the pyramid where the Ancients dumped large numbers of discarded bodies after rituals and feedings, suddenly spewed out the ghosts of these victims. Their forms looked decayed and grotesque, true to death, skeletal faces with no eyes. They were armed with razor-like swords and daggers, forged from the underworld. They were as skilled at fighting as those of the resistance. Their advantage was gliding over the ground or propelling through the air since they were spirit beings. The rule of gravity did not apply to them. They could gang up and easily overcome the fiercest vampire. The brotherhood stood in shock at witnessing this spiritual phenomenon, but they quickly came to see that they were on the same side. Together the brotherhood and the ghosts joined forces to do battle with their enemies.

Vampires came from all directions out of the jungle, the city, and the pyramid to do battle in the streets of Coba. Some of the vampires had decorative masks and dark robes, Zafrina's Ancients. The Ancients also had talismans to protect them from the sun, gifts for their devotion to the Dark One. The rest of the vampires were Zafrina's foot soldiers which had no talismans to protect them from sunlight. Whether it was poor planning or their over confidence, the vampires had to make a swift victory in order to beat the rising sun. But Zafrina cared nothing for her foot soldiers. They were expendable pawns in her lust for power.

Dark threatening clouds seemed to be gathering above the pyramid and expand to blanket the city. The thick clouds would prove to aid the vampire foot soldiers to fight in the daylight. Flickers of lightening appeared directly above the pyramid followed by rumbles of thunder. Zafrina was up to her tricks. It turns out that she would protect her army for the moment when it served her purpose.

The ghosts and humans worked together to rid the vampires by stabbing them through the heart or beheading them or both. Coba had become one big street fight where the winner takes all.

Melanna and Tez fought closely together, taking on the elite vampire soldiers. An Ancient challenged her as he stood there with his sleek muscular body peeking out of his dark robe that was blowing in the wind.

"I'll have your head on a stick before this is over, pretty princess," the Ancient hissed at her.

"And I'll have your talisman as a souvenir if I have any say in it. Take your best shot."

The sound of steel could be heard as the vampire unsheathed his sword. Melanna twirled her sword like a baton and continued to be in constant motion, both her sword and her body. Steel clashed with steel. It was a dance of death, beautiful but deadly. Melanna came so close to the Ancient that she was able to deliver a sharp elbow to the side of his face, unmasking him. The mask clattered to the ground and broke into pieces. He shook his head, only feeling it for a moment and smiled at her with an ugly monstrous smile. His face was pasty white and wrinkled. His black eyes stared unblinking like a snake stalking its prey. They continued to duel until she stopped for a split second to deliver the fatal stab of her sword, sending pure deathly Power through her enemy. After the body hit the ground, she made good on her promise as she walked over to the dead vampire, retrieved the talisman, and tucked it away for safe keeping.

Tez was confident that Melanna could handle herself. Every now and then his eyes flickered to see her doing battle. He only stopped once to do a surprise kill on a vampire that

Melanna was fighting when she had tripped and fallen over a dead body. After each kill, another vampire would come out of nowhere to take its place. Melanna continued fighting off the enemy, showing great skill and courage.

The resistance and their ghostly comrades fought their way inside the pyramid where vampires continued to flow out in large numbers. Where were all of these vampires coming from? Wave after wave of vampires seemed to be coming from deep below the pyramid.

Fighting in the streets raged on. Xoco and Manny decided to stay near Amoxtli during the battle. They felt a sense of protection and leadership with him close by. But that didn't mean it was easier for them. The vampires tried to take Amoxtli out since they knew how important he was to the resistance. That meant that Xoco and Manny had to fight that much harder than ever before. As a big burly vampire took Xoco to the ground while baring his fangs, some revenge-seeking ghosts tackled him and laid waste to him by stabbing him through the heart. Another plunged a sword through the vampire's head and cut it in half like a melon. Xoco felt queasy seeing that, but there was no time to linger on it. Manny needed her help.

Two vampires were being held off by Manny until Xoco reached him. She leaped into the air as she spun a full revolution with her sword tucked against her body. As she landed on her feet, she brought her sword into the back of one of Manny's attackers, piercing his heart. Manny and Xoco fought back to back as they continued to fight for their lives and their freedom. For every vampire they killed, there was always another one to take its place, and many more yet to come. How long could they keep this up?

Amoxtli, on the other hand, seemed to be enjoying the excitement of the battle. All these years cooped up in his temple, he hadn't seen this kind of action in a very long time. You could hear him laughing and challenging the vampires in the name of the Great Spirit. With his bone dagger in one hand and his long staff in the other, he fought off hordes of vampires, whirling to and fro like a human tornado. When the numbers were too many, he would simply slam the end of his staff on the ground and send a wave of Power coursing through the bodies of the monstrous beings. They fell where they stood. The vampire foot soldiers continued to advance on Amoxtli, their numbers twice as large as before.

Vengeful ghosts surrounded the foot soldiers from behind, cutting them through with their razor edged swords. They too fell to the ground.

A shout of victory rose from the humans, with Amoxtli holding his staff in the air.

There was suddenly a huge bonfire in the street at the foot of the pyramid. As the resistance steadily gained ground in their battle, the ghosts tossed limbs, torsos and heads of defeated vampires into the bonfire. It was like watching a sports game as body parts were thrown into the air and intercepted by the ghosts as they raced through the air and tossed them into the fire. Some ghosts could even be seen high-fiving each other in victory before racing back for more.

The resistance fought their way down into the belly of the pyramid, through the endless stream of the demonic beings, down winding stairs and dark corridors. They finally reached what appeared to be the ground level of the pyramid. To their surprise there was an endless pit from which vampires continued to crawl out of. Some gaped at the pit, wondering if their own struggle was all in vain. After all, who could win complete victory over an endless supply of undead vampires from what seemed like hell itself? Members of the brotherhood tried to use arrows to discourage any more from climbing up from the pit. There were sounds of torment and a putrid smell that came from the pit that was enveloped in darkness.

Tez took a torch from one of his comrades and dropped it into the pit as everyone watched until it could be seen no more. A few vampires could be seen trying to climb up as the light of the torch fell into nothingness.

Melanna pointed her sword toward the pit and raised her free hand in the air as she called upon the Great Spirit to end the terror of Zafrina's vampire army. Her dancing eagle cuff bracelet glowed in response. An explosion of white light filled the room with a rush of wind. Melanna's sword glowed and gathered a ball of white light. It sent a giant lightning bolt down into the endless pit, charring all bodies within it for miles.

"I want this pit sealed immediately so we don't have to deal with any more of these blood suckers than we already have running around now."

A group of strong men found some pillars to lay across the opening of the pit. They then brought some heavy stone statues to pile on top of those. Other people looked around to add to the pile. The humans were finally satisfied that no more vampires could make their way out.

The resistance and the ghostly army continued to fight their way throughout the pyramid, ridding every room of the undead. They came across a room that would be considered a kitchen. Human heads lined the shelves. Body parts hung from hooks. And there were giant urns of blood, urns that would normally store wine. The room reeked of rotting flesh. Everyone covered their faces to keep from breathing in the stench and continued on.

The resistance worked their way to the top of the pyramid and ended up outside under the stormy sky. There at the top in between the columns stood Zafrina with a group of beautiful seductive vampires, hissing and taking a defensive stance. At seeing the advancing humans, Zafrina caused a rush of wind to blow against them. Suddenly several ritualistic knives took to flight in the wind. Melanna's shield and helmet deflected these. Some of her comrades were not as fortunate as they crumpled to the ground. The humans came closer.

The fire from giant fire urns gathered strength to burn the humans as a wall of fire. The ghost warriors came forward to shield the humans from Zafrina's attempts to burn them alive. This only angered the Dark One. The humans and ghost warriors came even closer.

The beautiful vampires, recognizing the impending danger, leaped from the pyramid to the ground below. They disappeared into the jungle.

Zafrina stood her ground. The sky became angrier as it reflected the emotions that she felt in that moment. The clouds became even darker and moved in a circular motion above the pyramid.

Two Ancients entered the scene bringing a man with a sack over his head. They stopped in between the humans and Zafrina. To Melanna's horror, when one of them pulled the sack off of the man's head, it was none other than her father, king Tetaneeka. A few gasps could be heard from the resistance.

"Don't harm my father. I'll trade you my life for his. Just don't harm him, please."

Tez came forward to stand beside Melanna saying, "You'll do no such thing, not while I'm breathing."

"What makes you think that I value your life above his?"

Zafrina looked at her with disdain. And then she turned her attention to Tez.

"You look very familiar to me, although it has been many years ago. Tezcatli, isn't it? I would've never guessed that you would join up with these weak humans. They are nothing more than cattle to me."

"Yes, well, too bad I didn't have any stakes with me the day that we met. I would've put them to good use."

"You dare to defy me and turn against your own kind? You could've been a king in my world."

"I have no interest in sharing anything with you. You took everything from me, everyone that I've ever loved! I won't let that happen ever again."

Tez took Melanna's hand as she leaned into him for protection. Zafrina noticed the gesture and she smiled with evil delight.

"Well, it seems that I've arrived at an opportune time again in your life. What a coincidence."

"History will not repeat itself today. I can assure you of that. This time I will see that you get the death you deserve just like your beloved Lord Chak."

Zafrina's face became contorted with pain at hearing the truth about Chak's demise.

"If that is indeed true," she hissed, "then I will make you suffer beyond your imagination for what you've done."

Zafrina turned and picked up a spear to hurl not at Tez, but she took aim at Melanna. Tetaneeka sensing danger to his daughter ran to shield his daughter from the spear as it plunged into his stomach. A scream rose up from members of the resistance. Melanna bent over with great agony and shock, clutching at her father as he lay dying. Zafrina turned to flee to a better vantage point to defend herself and what was left of her army.

"Father!"

In a very weak voice he responded, "Melanna, I'm happy that I've made amends with you and that my last act as a father was protecting my daughter." A painful spasm racked his body as he clutched the spear's shaft.

"Father, save your strength."

He looked at her with peaceful eyes and said, "I'm sorry that it took me this long to finally admit that I love you and I have been blessed. I'm very proud of you for how you are fighting for your people. Something that I failed to do. I will always love you, please remember that." He let out a gasp of air and then he was gone with his eyes staring blankly at nothing. The tears rushed down Melanna's cheeks at having witnessed her father's death.

While Tetaneeka's life ebbed away, Tez rushed forward to do battle with Zafrina who clearly had the elements on her side. A column of dark clouds wrapped around them both and transported them to a high plateau on a large hill that stood adjacent to the pyramid. Once away from everyone else, they were free to battle to the death. Zafrina's robe flew about her as she lashed out with her sword at Tez. He was a very worthy opponent in her eyes. It would be a shame to kill him. But still, it had to be done. Their images blurred as they moved about the plateau in the dance of death, using every means against the other. The clashing of swords could be heard, thudding noises, crunching noises. Neither of them could gain the upper hand over the other nor would they yield one to the other. Suddenly it occurred to Zafrina that she could put an end to this and not have to kill Tez. She reached into the folds of her clothing and pulled out a six-pointed throwing star that she had picked up in her travels around the world. It had magical properties to it. She kicked a large tree in Tez's direction to buy her a few seconds.

She held the star to her lips and whispered, "Sleep and forget."

Tez cleared the tree out of his path. The moment that was done, he looked in her direction only to be struck in the forehead with the throwing star. He immediately crumpled to the ground. Zafrina turned to look at Melanna who was standing over her father's body. Melanna looked in disbelief at the form of her love on the ground. This couldn't be happening. She refused to believe it. A scream of grief escaped her lips like no other noise that was heard in the battle. To her it was as if she was hearing someone else scream in agony. The screaming turned into sobbing.

Zafrina smiled in satisfaction, thinking that she struck at the very heart of the resistance. She may have lost most of her vampires, but she single handedly took out the king and Tez as well as made Melanna suffer great grief. It was music to her ears.

Melanna abruptly stopped sobbing and looked around her, realizing that she had to pull herself together to finish this fight. Her grief turned to anger. Her anger turned into energy to finish off her enemy. She pounced on the closest vampire atop the pyramid, ramming her sword through it and decapitating it. She flung his head into the jungle. She moved like a mad woman, not able to get enough vampires to kill. She didn't need an army, not at this speed.

Finally, Melanna reached the top of the hill where Tez laid on the ground. Zafrina waited expectantly for her. Melanna stood there, breathing heavily after having killed so many vampires and climbing the hill. The princess and the Dark One circled each other. Finally Melanna struck out with her sword but wasn't able to combat Zafrina as she had the other vampires. The Dark One was faster at dodging the sword. She unleashed some hail and fire upon Melanna who stood her ground. The hail and fire bounced off her as if she stood under some protection. Thanks to her helmet.

Melanna thought better of doing quick maneuvers and decided to let the sword work for her. She raised her cuff bracelet towards the sky and entreated the Great Spirit to defeat the Dark One. A ball of bright light gathered in the sword and a sudden giant bolt of lightning hit Zafrina in the chest. She remained transfixed as she writhed in pain, screaming at the top of her lungs. Her flesh melted from her, exposing her bones.

Then suddenly her bones and her cape flew up into the swirling angry clouds. She was defeated but not entirely gone. Her power was broken over the city of Coba.

Melanna stood there watching the clouds. For a split second she thought that all of her enemies were vanquished, when suddenly she was struck from behind with a sword and run through from back to front where the breastplate did not protect her. One of the beautiful vampires that had leaped from the pyramid had come out of hiding and had done Zafrina's dirty work.

Blackness overtook Melanna. She could feel her body being dragged and finally dumped into the same mass grave that held the sacrificed humans.

20. THE AFTERMATH

A time to weep and a time to laugh, a time to mourn and a time to dance. Ecc. 3:4

The muffled sounds of the battle could be heard behind the pyramid where Melanna was now laying face down among the corpses in the mass grave. Her sword and shield were gone. She still wore her helmet and breastplate. Then the sound of rain seemed to drown out all the other noises. She experienced a feeling of being lifted into someone's arms, out of the stench of death and decay. Her heart beat ever so slowly. She felt as if she were floating away into nothingness except for a small string of life that was held by someone or something else at the other end, keeping her in her body a bit longer. She felt as though she were flying through the air, her hair and clothes rustled in the wind. She heard the distinct sound of huge wings beating the air. The body that held her felt so warm, his fragrance so pleasant to inhale. When Melanna tried to open her eyes the tiniest bit, she saw nothing but light.

"Stay with me, princess. We're almost there."

The force was getting much stronger to be sucked away. The string of life was tight but strong. How strong was she? How strong was her will to live? Finally she floated down gently. Her gear was taken off of her. Then she felt his hands on her back and stomach where the sword had been driven through her. A sensation of heat radiated from that touch and coursed throughout her body.

Melanna fell into a peaceful sleep. Micah looked down at her with satisfaction of knowing he had saved her from certain death. This one act should put him in good standing with the Great Spirit. But there was much more work to be done. And more places to visit.

The pace of the battle dwindled down as the last of the vampires were eradicated from the streets of Coba. After the last vampire in the street was put to death, Amoxtli and the resistance stood facing their ghostly comrades. Some living members of the resistance recognized their departed family members or friends. With tears in their eyes they waved to them, pledging their undying love to them as they said goodbye. A great wind signaled the departure of the ghosts as they disappeared to the other side, into eternity.

The people of Coba now turned to the task of cleaning up the city as they put the last remains of vampires into the bonfire. Comrades who were dead were gathered and placed for proper burial.

The day was swiftly coming to an end. Up on the high plateau of the hill that was adjacent to the pyramid, Tez became conscious as he lay on the ground and looked up into the starry sky. How had he gotten there? What was this thing sticking out of his forehead?

The beautiful vampire that had run Melanna through with a sword was sitting in the shadows and waiting for Tez to become conscious. Her name was Teora. She was in Zafrina's inner circle that was loyal to her interests. Her features hinted at a Polynesian origin with her tawny skin, flowing dark hair that stopped at her waist, and dark almond eyes that were set in an oval face. Zafrina had named her Teora when she made her into a vampire, which means "life". It was fitting name for an immortal starting out in her new life. Before she was a vampire, her people had sacrificed her to the sharks which they worshiped as gods. Zafrina smelled the blood and ran several miles before seeing the staked body in the water with the cloud of blood around her. She fed Teora her own blood just before she died from her wounds. She remembered very little about her past life, even her own name. This is why Teora welcomed a new name from her maker. They shared a very strong bond. Teora was faithful to the Dark One even when it seemed as though Zafrina was gone forever. But the bones of Zafrina, the essence of her called out to Teora.

Tez sat up and looked around. By that time Teora was standing at his side with a hand to help him to his feet.

"What is this thing in my forehead? And how did it get there?"

"You must've been playing with the wrong people. Don't you remember anything?"

"Not a thing!" Then he eyed the beautiful vampire and asked, "I'm sorry. Do I know you?"

Teora recognized the opportunity to make up an elaborate lie. She could make Tez do whatever she wanted and he wouldn't be the wiser.

"Come now, Tezcatli! Don't be a tease! You don't recognize a friend when you see one? It's me, Teora."

She stood in front of Tez, grabbed the throwing star and yanked it out. The wound immediately started to close up. She flung the weapon to the ground and slapped her hands together as if getting rid of some imaginary dirt.

"How many times have I told you not to play with such things?"

"Why don't I remember anything? Or even know who I am?"

Tez studied the cuff bracelets he wore with the dancing eagle as he fingered the stamped image. They didn't spark any memory for him.

"Don't worry. It may come back to you. Just be patient. What is the last thing that you remember anyway?"

Tez walked over to a sword on the ground and picked it up. There it was again on the hilt of the sword: a dancing eagle. This was no ordinary sword. He stuck it into the ground forming a cross. Perhaps the owner would see it here and retrieve it.

"I can remember little snap shots of a beautiful woman and a waterfall. That was when I was mortal. I think I remember my mother and father, but it's so hard..." he put a fist to his head as he tried to make himself remember.

"Don't worry yourself right now-"

"Wait. There was a woman giving birth under a tree...when I was a vampire. Why can't I remember?"

"Come on, Tezcatli! We have bigger problems to deal with. We happen to be passing through a city that is at war with vampires. If they spot us, they will kill us! So we have to be careful in getting out of here."

Teora walked over to the sword and tried to grasp the hilt. It burned her with Power preventing her from taking it from its place. She shook and rubbed her hand from the exchange. Tez didn't seem to notice in his confusion.

Teora took Tez by the arm as they both crouched low to the ground at the edge of the plateau. They took a moment to watch the humans below as they cleaned up the city after the battle.

When they had enough of watching the humans, Tez asked, "Why were we even traveling through this city?"

"We were supposed to meet with your beloved Zafrina. And don't tell me that you don't remember her."

"Sorry, I don't," he said as he scratched his head. "Who is she?"

"She has been your companion and lover for the past two hundred years. I suggest that you try to remember that really fast. You don't want to hurt her feelings."

"Okay, so why isn't she here?"

"Zafrina ran into some big trouble with princess Melanna of Coba. Melanna tried to kill her, to extinguish her life force. But I feel Zafrina's presence inside of me. I hear her calling to me, beckoning me to make the journey to find her. We need to make the journey together to find and restore her to her former glory. She needs you."

The mention of Melanna's name didn't faze Tez. She was lost to him in his forgetfulness. Tez followed Teora down the steep hill. When they reached the bottom of the hill, they thought that they were alone. They soon discovered that they were mistaken.

Manny was searching for Melanna. He knew that she was in this vicinity. When he rounded a corner that his vision was partially blocked by palms and trees, Tez and Teora came into view.

"Hey, Tez. I wondered where you had gotten too. I saw you way up on that high plateau earlier kicking some serious butt-"

Teora stepped in front of Tez in a crouching form, hissing and baring her fangs. By that time Xoco, who had not been trailing too far away from Manny, came to stand next to him. She stood there with her eyes wide with surprise and her mouth open, but just for an instant. Her fighter instinct kicked into gear as she unsheathed her sword and took a fighting stance. Teora knew better than to meet a challenge right now. She grabbed Tez's arm and ran into the jungle with him at great speed, only seen as a blur.

"Who was that?" Manny asked in bewilderment.

"I don't know. I've never seen her before. Zafrina must have kept her well hidden."

"What do you make of Tez just standing there, letting her do that?"

"It's safe to say that he isn't himself. Something must have happened to him during the battle. We had better tell Amoxtli right away."

* * * * *

Back at the palace, the servants were preparing a funeral for their beloved king. They were all in great mourning.

Melanna continued to rest in bed. When she woke up and looked across her room, Qaileen was asleep in a chair not far from Melanna's bed. Qaileen swatted at a fly which roused from her sleep.

"Oh, child, how do you feel? We were afraid that we had lost you."

"I actually feel pretty good considering that I remember being run through with a sword."

She reached behind her to inspect the wound. Since she was unable to reach it, Qaileen came to lift up Melanna's garment to inspect it. To her surprise, she saw no such wound, only smeared blood and blood on some of her garments.

"By the gods! You have been healed!" She sat on the bed and embraced Melanna with the tenderness of a mother. "Do you remember what happened?"

"I remember that someone dragged me and threw me into that wretched mass grave near the pyramid. And then I felt myself being transported here, as though I were flying. I know that sounds insane."

"Well, I saw the young man who brought you here, you know, the one covered in tattoos?"

"Micah?"

"And believe me, he doesn't look like a healer. And when you see him next time, can you please tell him to stop leaving a trail of black feathers on the floor? I can't keep this place clean as it is without someone deliberately doing that!"

Melanna smiled to herself. She was starting to realize who Micah really was. She needed to see Amoxtli and tell him what she knew about him. Then a great sadness fell over Melanna as she remembered seeing the death of her father.

"What have they done with father's body?"

Qaileen took Melanna's hand, squeezed it and said, "Oh, little one, I'm so sorry for your loss. They have placed his body on his bed for now. His servants, advisors and closest friends have come here to grieve for him before formal funeral plans have been made."

Melanna said nothing in answer, but only nodded her head.

Later that evening, when all of the guests had left the palace, Melanna slipped into her father's bed chamber to say her own goodbyes to him. Many candles were lit, bathing him in golden light. He was dressed in a shimmering robe. His hands were placed on top of his stomach. He looked like he was sleeping peacefully. She squeezed his cold hand and placed a kiss upon his bearded cheek.

"Life has been so unfair to us, hasn't it, father?" Half expecting him to reply to her, she began to cry, wishing that her father could embrace her in that moment and knowing that he never would again. But in that same moment, a ray of hope filled her heart in knowing that his spirit flew like an eagle to be with the Great Spirit. He was really no longer here. He was soaring above, looking down on her, cheering her on to continue on her path of life. She took comfort in knowing that.

"I will miss you, father. I will try to live my life in such a way that I would make you proud of me. And tell mother that her little girl is all grown up now," she said with a bit of a smile, but tears clouded her eyes. After a moment longer of reflection and tears, she left Tetaneeka's room and walked to her own room.

Upon entering her room, she realized that this was really no longer her room. She was a married woman. Her life was with Tez now, whatever that life entailed. Well, she did say those marriage vows even though it wasn't to the person that was supposed to be standing next to her. And she did have a honeymoon, she just didn't dream about it. Where was her beloved? Why wasn't he here?

She went to her window to scan the trees and the ground below. Worry grew stronger in her heart. She quickly dressed and put on a hooded robe to go to Amoxtli's temple.

The streets of Coba were void of traffic. The faint sounds of children in their homes could be heard, carried on the balmy wind. Melanna walked swiftly to her destination. The last rays of the sun were disappearing on the horizon when she entered the Temple of the Brotherhood of the Eagle. Melanna stood there for a moment, looking around when her eyes fell on Amoxtli, Xoco and Manny. They stopped talking when she entered the temple, all eyes on her. She threw back her hood and joined them as they all greeted her with hugs.

Amoxtli began by asking, "What happened to you today? It was as if you disappeared right under our noses."

"I was fighting Zafrina, giving her all I had. It wasn't enough. I finally just let the Power of the sword work for me. The last time I saw her, her bones and her cape went swirling up into the storm clouds."

"Awesome! I hope that's the last we see of her!" Manny smiled.

"But to my horror, a few seconds later I was run through by a sword. I never saw who did it."

"No doubt one of Zafrina's vampires that we missed," said Amoxtli as he nodded.

"The next thing I know is that someone tosses me in the mass grave."

"But how could you be standing here if this person gave you a fatal wound?"

"I suspect that I have received supernatural healing through a young man named Micah." She rolled her eyes and said, "He's our mystery traveler that is employed as a gardener at the palace. Qaileen said that he brought me to the palace. Have you heard of him?"

With a smile on his lips, Amoxli replied, "Actually, yes. I know him very well. I first met him in my younger days when I was training to be a priest. On my way home one night, a robber stabbed me, took my money, and left me to die in the street. I could feel my life slipping away. I felt a sensation of flying in the arms of an angel, of healing energy bursting through me. When I opened my eyes, a man with deep coppery hair and blue eyes said I would be okay. I wanted to know more about him and what I had experienced. We spent the entire night talking about things unseen and about things yet to come. He said that his mission here among us is not to be a champion of mankind against the evils of this world, but to warn us of things to come and to bring healing wherever he can."

"I wonder why he couldn't bring healing to my father in his time of need."

"Micah can't foresee everything. You're father was already gone by the time he could've helped him anyway. And there were far too many people present. Angels, if I may use that term, tend to work mostly under cover, not revealing their true nature."

"Do you think he possesses any abilities to help find lost people? Amoxtli shrugged at her question. "Where is Tez? He should be here. Has anyone seen him?"

"That's what we've been talking to Amoxtli about. Manny and I saw Tez at the foot of the tall hill near the pyramid. He was with another vampire that we've never seen before."

"Ya, Tez didn't even acknowledge me when I spoke to him, like he didn't know me. The female vampire crouched in a fighting position before she saw Xoco was with me. Then she took Tez by the arm and ran into the jungle." Manny looked adoringly at Xoco and said, "She was afraid of you, babe," as he stroked her arm.

"Something tells me that wasn't the case," said Amoxtli, "as much as I'd like to give Xoco credit. The vampire must have wanted to get Tez away from here rather than have a confrontation with humans."

"But aren't we going after him? What are we going to do?" Melanna questioned Amoxtli.

"Let me entreat the Great Spirit on this matter. Go home for now. I'll speak with you about this tomorrow."

Melanna reluctantly did as Amoxtli said. It was dark anyway. There was nothing that could be done at that moment.

It was a long night. Melanna had fitful dreams about the vampire war of Coba and about seeing her father speak to her in his last moments. His lips moved but she couldn't hear him. Tez was fighting Zafrina in the distance. She ran to her love to aid him in the fight. Her feet were heavy as she ran in slow motion. Darkness seemed to want to swallow her and the trees seemed to close her in. When she stood at his side, he turned his head to look down into her eyes. It wasn't Tez who held her. It was Chak with a pasty dead face with part of his skull exposed through rotting flesh. He opened his mouth to bite her. Zafrina laughed her loud devilish laugh.

A clap of thunder boomed above and shook the ground. Melanna shook the bed with a start and opened her eyes from her dream. It was raining outside. It was raining on her love who was somewhere in the jungle.

Why won't you come to me, Tez?

* * * * *

After much prayer, Amoxtli retired for the night and had his own dreams.

"Give me a sign," he pleaded at the end of his prayer.

Amoxtli dreamed that a giant eagle swooped out of the sky to perch on top of the pyramid. The pyramid cracked with a huge fissure under the eagle's weight. Then the great bird devoured the bodies of the enemy until it was full and flew away. His dream took him to the ocean in the Northern Yucatan where a Spanish galleon set sail for the New World across the Gulf of Mexico. An unearthly force intruded on the scene as a terrible storm formed endangering the ship. Evil eyes were staring from the monstrous clouds. Next his dream took him to a beach of white sand. The native people were strange looking with their different jewelry, clothing, and adornment of feathers. They looked angry as they discovered foreigners invading their territory. Then huge waves of Spaniards and dark skinned natives clashed in the strange flat land. They kept running in waves to combat each other to the death. The blood flowed and the bodies stacked up in a high mound in the flat beautiful wilderness. And then the Spaniards rolled a huge elongated metal object into the battle, placed a large metal ball into it, and then a deafening explosion was heard. Amoxtli opened his eyes with a start. He was troubled by the dream. But the Great Spirit would guide his thoughts to interpret it.

The next morning when Amoxtli readied himself for a new day, Manny stopped in to talk to Amoxtli.

"Good morning, Amoxtli. I hope you slept better than me last night. That thunderstorm kept me awake."

"I did sleep some, but I do recall a few thunder boomers."

"Did you hear?"

"Hear what?"

"The pyramid. There is a huge fissure in it from the top the bottom. Everyone is saying that it is a sign from above. What do you make of it?"

"Funny you should ask. I had a dream about that last night," Amoxtli said as he rubbed his chin trying to remember. "If that came true, I wonder if the rest of my dream will come true as well."

"What? You have a gift of foresight?"

"I asked the Great Spirit for a sign last night. He didn't disappoint. But I really must talk to Melanna as soon as I can."

* * * * *

The news spread rapidly throughout the Mayan empires in other provinces of king Tetaneeka's death. They came with haste to the City of Coba. Tetaneeka's body was laid out for public viewing for one day outside of the tomb he would be buried in. People from other Mayan cities that knew him or did business with him were there out of respect. So many people wanted to catch their final glimpse of Tetaneeka that Coba was bursting at the seams. The city was hardly large enough for such a turn out.

The following day at noon, Tetaneeka's body was carried on the shoulders of some brawny Mayan men through the streets and to the final resting place. Hordes of people followed behind the funeral procession, crying and bearing gifts of flowers and trinkets to leave for their beloved king. Tetaneeka was laid to rest in a lavish tomb next to his beloved Almika. Amoxtli said some comforting words to the vast crowd, assuring them that their king was looking down on them and ultimately in the presence of the Great Spirit.

After the musicians played, as with their tradition, they broke their instruments and placed them inside the tomb. People brought their gifts of pottery, jade, obsidian, shells and other beautiful trinkets to be placed in Tetaneeka's tomb as well.

Some men took some of the king's servants and forced them to their knees to be sacrificed and to accompany their king in death, to serve him in the afterlife. Amoxtli stayed their hands. He declared that the people would no longer take innocent life as they had seen the vampires do these many months. They were all free men under the same sky, all brothers under the watchful eye of the Great Spirit. The vast crowd slowly dispersed.

Amoxtli accompanied Melanna to the palace where he spent some time with her. She looked weary having not slept much during the night. Amoxtli told her everything in his dream. He believed that Tez had left the country by ship, bound for the New World. She would go to him. She would make the trip alone if she had to. Tez had been her destiny from the beginning. There was no denying that. And her purpose was not yet fulfilled, at least not in her mind.

"You said it yourself at my father's funeral, 'we are all free men under the same sky, all brothers under the watchful eye of the Great Spirit '. If you really meant what you said, then I am renouncing the throne and all rights to rule over the people of Coba. This should be a nation of free men, not to be dictated to by a few. So I will entrust the leadership to you as the people of Coba move forward. I trust that you will put people in place that will lead them and get them back on track."

Amoxtli was taken aback at her words. It came as a shock, but shock quickly turned to love and courage. He felt he was up to the task of this part of the rebuilding process as he nodded to her in agreement.

"Good. Now that that's settled, we need to come up with a plan. And we need to know who is going with me on this trip."

"Are you sure you are up for this? Are you willing to sacrifice everything to go after him?"

"He would've done the same for me. I love him. We belong to each other. I simply can't live without him."

Amoxtli nodded as he looked into her eyes.

"There is a very old book that I would like you to see. I came to realize that a passage is written in there that reveals the origin of Zafrina. But it's in the temple among the relics."

"May I see it now?"

"Certainly! Let's go."

They left the palace together and walked to the Temple of the Eagle. The Eternal Flame was still burning at the entrance. The manicured shrubs stood like little centuries. They walked into the temple which was beginning to feel hot since it was almost mid day. The heat from the hundreds of candles accentuated the feeling. Melanna and Amoxtli stood at the shelves of ancient artifacts. He took the old book "The Fall of Man & the Promise of the Great Spirit" and opened it to a passage near the beginning of the book.

"I didn't realize that this ancient writing spoke of the beginning of Zafrina's reign of terror until after the battle. It was the strangest thing. I came in here as usual to say my daily prayers at the altar, when all of the sudden a great wind came through here. The wind picked the book off the shelf and opened it to this passage. It was as if the Great Spirit revealed this to me Himself."

Melanna was speechless but waited for him to go on.

Amoxtli read to her from the book. Hundreds of years ago, when the Egyptians had enslaved the Jewish race, Zafrina was among the Egyptian leaders who lorded over the slaves. Back then she was just as evil, delighting in the death or the torture of the slaves. She couldn't get enough of it. One day, Zafrina decided to force the Jewish slaves to worship the giant gods of stone that they had been forced to make. The slaves refused since their God forbade them to do such things. Zafrina threatened to kill twelve of their priests, twelve being the number of tribes that made up the Jewish nation. Still the slaves would not bow. One by one Zafrina removed the pumping heart from each priest while they were still alive long enough to see it being done. The screams could be heard from all over the city. After the twelfth priest lay dead, Zafrina carried the hearts of the priests into the Jew's place of worship, into the Most Holy Place. It was there that she threw the hearts on the altar, daring to defy their God. The chamber filled with the smoke of the angry God. A thunderous voice from heaven condemned Zafrina to be cursed and walk the earth, unable to quench her thirst for blood. The earth trembled at His voice. Zafrina felt the weight of her condemnation and screamed as if she endured physical pain. Dark swirling clouds and bolts of lightning filled the sky above her. Zafrina's personal servants became as dead men with translucent skin, under the same curse as their leader. These would be known as the Ancients. That is why they roamed the earth from one nation to another, unable to quench their fiery thirst. Wherever they traveled, she would make the people of each nation they visited to build a monument for her such as the great pyramid of Coba. It seemed that the world did not hold enough life for them to consume.

"So you can see why she was such a formidable enemy. I don't think that we've seen the last of her. You saw it yourself. She was taken up into the clouds, no doubt to be empowered and come back again."

"That is why I need you to teach me what you know. I need you to prepare me for my quest, to end her once and for all and to rescue Tez."

Outside the temple, the storm clouds were clearing from the sky at a slow pace with warm breezes from the Caribbean Sea. The jungle was once again filled with the songs of hundreds of birds, the large cats hunted their prey, and the rest of the animals went on as if nothing had ever occurred to hinder the cycle of life as it had always been and always will be in the Yucatan.

EPILOGUE - THE NEW WORLD

Across the waters of the Gulf of Mexico, in the territory of old Florida, a dark spiritual being was flung into the murky Everglades, born on the winds of hurricane-like storm clouds. It would appear to be only a human skeleton beneath a cape to the human eye. But at closer inspection, the bones moved to snatch up any living creature to feed on its blood. With each animal or reptile fed upon, ligaments formed to the bones, muscle formed over bones, skin formed over muscle, and long dark hair flowed past her shoulders. Days passed as this process went on, but some animals were too cautious to enter her domain as if they could sense the evil spirit that lurked there. The chances of Everglade creatures wandering into the space of the Dark One was taking too long. She needed victims to regain her strength and beauty.

Many days passed until one day the Dark One peeked in between the sawgrass to see some young Indian boys passing through. There was hope for her yet as she planned to attack and feed once again. She made a moaning sound. The two boys heard it and walked close to her. They took in her emaciated putrefied skin and elegant cape.

"Wow, what do you think happened here?" said the first boy.

"I don't know but I think we should get out of here!" replied his friend.

And before either of them could make a move, Zafrina reached out and grabbed the ankle of the first boy who began screaming and struggling. His friend was so terrified that he fled back home to his tribe. With fangs extended, Zafrina plunged them into the boy's neck and drained him completely of his blood. Almost instantly, Zafrina's youthful appearance was restored. She dropped the limp body and stood on her feet.

"Delicious! I think that I'm going to like it here."

About the Author

Glenda Reynolds currently resides in the Florida Panhandle with her husband of 29 years. She also works at a full time job and only does writing on the side. Another book is in the works as we follow Melanna on her journey to find her lost love, Tez.

http://glendareynolds.blogspot.com/

http://facebook.com/glenda.g.reynolds

Made in the USA
Charleston, SC
08 October 2012